I0788150

Mean, Median, and a Mostly Uninteresting GIRL

Mean, Median, and a Mostly Uninteresting GIRL

by

Cheyenne LaRoque

Parrhesia PUBLISHING

Copyright 2023 by
Cheyenne LaRoque, Mean, Median, and a Mostly Uninteresting Girl

All Rights Reserved
Published by Leadership Books, Inc. Las Vegas, NV – New York, NY
LeadershipBooks.com

ISBN:
978-1-951648-48-0 (Hardcover)
978-1-951648-50-3 (Paperback)
978-1-951648-51-0 (eBook)

Leadership Books, Inc is committed to publishing works of quality and integrity. In that spirit, we are proud to offer this book to our readers; however, the story, the experiences, and the words are the authors alone. The conversations in the book all come from the author's recollections, not word-for-word transcripts. All of the events are true to the best of the author's memory. The author, in no way, represents any company, corporation, or brand mentioned herein. The views expressed are solely those of the author.

Author's Dedication

For Grandpa, in hopes of making you proud.
For Grandma, the second half of my soul.

Table of Contents

Mean, Median, and a Mostly Uninteresting Girl

This isn't a suicide note.

If it was, it'd be the world's longest one.

No, instead, this is a story, my story,
and I'll tell it how I want it to be told.

Prologue

It's not like I haven't thought about it, killing myself. I think it's become normal to do so, expected even. There's nothing remarkable about it, this life and death pendulum that swings about in my head. Cracking the side of my own personal hourglass and letting the sand spill out has never been on my agenda but I can't say I don't think about dying.

I just don't think about how it's done or anything. No, I don't think about anything that grotesque. I prefer to contemplate the morbid.

What kind of flowers my mom would pick for the funeral; that's a thought that often pops into my mind. Who would actually bother to show up; that's something I'd really like to know. With the already massive and exponentially growing population of fake people in the world, I would assume only a tenth of the ones who allow the word friend to slip from their lips regarding me and my standing would be in attendance.

Oh, the movies I'd miss is another big one. The movies, the video games, the concerts, the songs, the little things that I take for granted in my life that I would be unable to experience when I was no longer living. It's morbid, honestly, thinking about death as a compilation of experiences I'd miss, but it's how I think about it. I promised myself one thing when it comes to whatever this is and it's that I'm not going to lie or sugarcoat it.

I've thought about dying, what's so bad about that? It's not like I've thought about being the one to end my own life, no, it's not like that. I've thought about dying in every other possible way. Car crash, heart attack, choking, struck by lightning, disemboweled by a shark, mauled by a bear, collapsing ceiling, crushed by a vending machine, you name it, I've imagined it. It's not so much a fantasy, but it's more of a "It wouldn't be so bad" sort of thought. A "Well I wouldn't exactly move out of the way of a falling vending machine," sort of thought, not a fantasy but a dark little slice of complacence towards mortality.

I know it's not healthy. I don't need to pay someone to tell me that, shit, I can take a Buzzfeed quiz to tell me that. The internet can probably diagnose me with whatever kind of chemical imbalance I likely have. I don't see any reason to talk to someone with a fancy degree. That's why I'm talking to you, and you really are as great a listener as I've been told. So, because you'll listen, here I am.

CHAPTER 1

The Beginning of the End

Iwas three weeks into my first year of college. I missed my high school friends, my drama club, my parents, my cats, and yes, even my brothers. I guess you don't really know about any of that, huh? Well, now is probably a better time than ever to get you acquainted with the mess of people, things, and experiences that compose my life.

I've always been completely, absolutely, entirely average. Even the day I was born was average. My mother had an average birth with an average amount of pain and absolutely no complications.

The beginning of my life was average and boring. I was 7.7 pounds exactly, which, unironically, is the average weight for a baby of European heritage. I had brown, dull, non-twinkling eyes that have followed me through each and whatever semblance of adulthood college acts I experienced, with hair the color of mud to match. My parents picked the only name to match my average existence: Jane.

It's not that I have anything against the name or even how extraordinarily ordinary I turned out to be, but I just find it all so unnecessarily on-brand. My name is probably my favorite part about myself. A lot of people jump straight to the most typical and boring nickname they can think of for me and so I have been dubbed Plain Jane by almost everyone (we'll get to those who are a little more creative in a moment). It's not exactly clever but it gets the point across, sure, yet I prefer a different name.

Jane Doe.

An admittedly morbid thought, but I believe that, were I to die, I'd initially be a Jane Doe. Unrecognizable not due to facial burning or missing prints or even just natural decomposition but instead due to my absolutely average appearance. I simply would be undistinguishable from every other Jane Doe brought into the morgue.

Even my parents would be unable to pick me out from the bunch and my grave would be filled with the remains of a total stranger. My mistaken remains would be the most interesting aspect of my life and they wouldn't even be mine. A morbid thought, sure, but a reoccurring one.

My family, unlike me, is anything but ordinary.

My mother is a real estate agent that deals exclusively in buildings that either were once horribly violent crime scenes or are believed to be haunted. Not exactly your everyday run-of-the-mill job but I suppose someone has to do it. She's got a real knack for convincing people that a past murder-suicide scene is the perfect environment for a new family and that the pets' specter chasing is endearing and will help them keep slim and fit without the constant need for neighborhood walks. I can't say I've taken too much of an interest in her work, but I definitely remember her excitement when she described finally handing off the keys to one of Thomas Sweatt's surviving arson attempts to an absolutely lovely set of newlyweds. She's exactly the perfect mix of quirky and creepy you would imagine necessary for such a unique job.

My father is a psychologist. Sounds normal enough, right? Well, I wasn't done. He's a *pet* psychologist. Yes, a psychologist for people's pets. Absurd, right?

To think he got a doctorate in psychology only to end up listening to the uninterpretable sounds of animals and trying to make some sort of sense of them. The things people will do for money, no matter how demeaning, are simply incredible to me. His job is no exception.

My brothers are equally as extraordinary. Being twins, their existence had already started off more interesting than mine. Not only were they twins, but one of them was unexpected.

My parents had been told they were going to have one child but ended up with two. My dad calls them the two for one duo. They had only picked out one name for a boy when they ended up with a spare so they did what any reasonable couple would do and named one of the twins after the first name they could think of.

Unfortunately, or fortunately, depending on your preferences, the first name they could think of came from the movie that was playing in the room where my parents waited until the contractions were close enough together. Perhaps *Psycho* isn't the best movie to be watching while preparing for birth but that's how I ended up with Desmond and Norman. Hopefully, the latter doesn't end up like his namesake, but only time will tell.

So far, neither of them seem very likely to be psychopaths, and, if they were, I'm sure my dad would be able to pick up on it. Well, maybe not; he could've lost his human touch after years of listening to the likely inexistent problems of his animal patients. But I don't think there's much to worry about with either of them. They've only just started their junior year of high school, and each of them has colleges throwing themselves at their feet. Desmond, being a junior Olympian, already has a mass of swimming scholarships being hurled his way. Norman, a three-time national Science Olympiad champ, has the likes of Harvard and Yale knocking down his door even though he's hoping to stay semi-local. He's worn a Johns Hopkins hoodie almost every day since sixth grade.

Meanwhile, I'm just me. Boring, average, Plain Jane with no extraordinary traits. My friends always tried to argue, but I knew they were just blowing smoke. No matter how many lies they tried to tell me, my friends were definitely the most extraordinary part about me.

Then college happened.

The first to leave was Thea.

Already, she sounds a million times more interesting than me with a name like that. We first met in the second grade when she moved back to her father's hometown after his time being stationed on military bases came to a close. She had brought Gushers to lunch, and I had never seen a fruit snack that looked so much like candy and currency at the same time. Thus friendship was set in stone.

Each conversation was always more interesting than the last when it came to Thea. One day we even got down to the nitty-gritty and discussed the fact that her name is a combination of two of the most used words in the English language. She's always pronounced her name, despite everyone's disagreement, as "Tay-uh." From that day on, "The-uh" became the name I used for her whenever she was being too dramatic, a tool I'd use to remind her of her simpler, more grounded roots.

And let me tell you, Thea put the dramatic in dramatic arts.

She was the one to convince me to join the drama club, after many months of pestering. It was in her treehouse where we both discovered our shared love of theatre, many years before high school, but she had always been more assured in her love. She was a playwright through and through, and it shone in her everyday life. Every action she took, every word that came out of her mouth, every reaction towards another soul, they were all parts of her internal, constantly-updating, unendingly-edited script.

I, however, was a guinea pig for her other works. She'd craft characters for me to become, and that's how I learned that I was much better at being anybody other than myself. Becoming a character was my way of becoming interesting and Thea was always ready to supply new ones. Sometimes, when we'd grab a coffee from our favorite little hole-in-the-wall café, aptly named Roast with the Most, she'd give me a character to play out as we ordered. The baristas became so accustomed to us and our games that they began naming drinks after every new character I stepped into as I stepped through the doors and chimed the bell.

The Karen, for example, was a large cup filled to the brim with espresso shots for the everyday stressed-out soccer mom, but it could only be ordered directly from the manager in the form of a complaint.

The Stacey McHotness was a pumpkin spice, half-caf, no whip, "skinny" yet somehow sugar coma-inducing latte for everyone's favorite prom queen.

The list goes on to cover all sorts of archetypes that Thea coined as her own. Once she finally dragged me to a drama club meeting with her, the skills I obtained from our foolish game became useful. Not only were they tools with which allowed me to get my name at the top of every playbill, but turned out to be the hammer and chisel that carved out many friendships.

The first of these friendships was with the Romeo to my Juliet in my first production.

Luckily for me, Edison Bishop was gay.

The lack of real-world romantic drama made it so easy for us to put chemistry on the stage. It sounds counterintuitive, yes, but think about it, without any real-life drama, the love and desire would be only beneath the lights and never behind the scenes. Our hearts, our desire, our romance was completely projected towards the audience, and they adored it. We had full house after full house for that production.

Thea was especially proud for being the one to cast the two of us and Mr. Mitchell could not have been more pleased with her choice and its outcome. After that massive success, she worked side by side with Mr. Mitchell in producing each show. Needless to say, when he finally came to her and asked her to produce one of her own original works, Eddie and I were her go-to leads.

He was the first to experience the brilliance that was and still is our Roast with the Most shenanigans. He was also the first to participate in them. Our drink was quickly named the Star-Crossed, for simply unimaginable reasons.

Edison, or Eddie as we affectionately called him, was best known for his outlandish auditions. His audition for Romeo is still our favorite conversation starter. He came to the audition dressed in full black, with his face adorned in only the finest of goth-themed makeup. He took quite a unique approach by making the love-struck Montague a full-on emo.

Thea was head-over-heels for this interpretation and Mr. Mitchell threw her a bone.

Last, but certainly not least in our ragtag group, was everyone's favorite theatrical power couple. Their names were no less perfect for each other than the people themselves. Valerie and Victor, or Val and Vic, were the on-again-off-again romantic time bomb that every drama club needs. They were as close to a fiery romance as two high schoolers could be, full of fights, break-ups, make-ups, make outs, betrayals, and the almost ancient boombox scene. That's right, at one point Vic stood outside of Val's window with a boombox to beg for forgiveness, and yes, before you ask, it was raining. I was the one who gave him a ride to her house, so I took the liberty of getting the whole thing on video and the file I have it saved under is still one of my most treasured pieces of blackmail.

The way we met these two was more of an unfortunate coincidence than anything. It was during one of their breakup phases that Valerie came into the dressing room where I was being bound in a corset by Thea. Valerie probably still ships Thane, or Jaea (however that would be pronounced) to this day, either way, she was in tears. While physically having the air pushed out of your lungs, the worst thing that could possibly happen is someone barging in and demanding you have a full-on, important conversation right at that exact moment.

Now, I'm not going to say this was my proudest moment, but I stripped off the corset after letting it fall to around my ankles and sat there listening to this girl, who I had not been previously acquainted with, rant about her relationship problems in nothing but my underwear and an open mind because, in that moment, who was I to judge? Thea did her best to fill in the various blanks of Valerie's story such as who she was, who Victor was, why she was crying, and basically everything else because, in all honesty, she was completely inarticulate in her rant.

Only later did I learn she was, surprisingly, the immaculately eloquent debate team captain and, far less surprisingly, a fantastic set designer.

Long story short, Thea and I managed to code break her choked-out story and track down Vic after I threw on my average tank top and running shorts. I thought it was all a downhill battle from there but oh how wrong I was. He was a mess all on his own.

Victor was busy staining his cheeks with black eyeliner tear streaks. He was deep in his goth phase at this point, thankfully he grew out of it as the years went on, but it was a less than pretty sight when I first laid my eyes on the gothic water fountain. It was as though a very lucky property owner struck oil directly beneath his eyelids. But I digress.

Thea and I discovered him hiding behind the science wing, beside a dumpster. (This safe place for breakdowns later became known as "Vic's Breakdown Bunker"). The sleeves of his black hoodie were smeared with white face paint. He was *very* deep in said goth phase. I couldn't help but chuckle at the lightning blue streak in his blonde hair, but Thea was kind enough to jab me in the side with her elbow before I could get a snide remark out.

After decoding his sniveled side of the story, we quickly learned that this would be the first of many stupid fights the two would have. Disputes over where to eat? Time to break up. Disagreement on what color is the best? Time to break up. Improper use of the word your/you're in a text? Time to break up.

The two were inseparable yet volatile for the longest time. Their unnecessary breakups became a bit of a game to Thea and me, as awful as that sounds. We'd place bets, most commonly the prize of a beverage of choice from the Roast, on if a stupid argument between the two would become an even more stupid breakup.

By the end of senior year, I had earned $573 worth of drinks thanks to their oil and vinegar dynamic.

Just as quickly as they had barged into our lives, they were in on our coffee shop hijinks. I even convinced our favorite barista to name a drink after Vic and Val. The Volatile was an avocado mocha frap with avocado whipped cream and a dark chocolate drizzle on top. They were two flavors that shouldn't taste great together but surprisingly worked, a perfect metaphor for their imperfect relationship.

Eventually, though, we all grew up in our own little ways. Unfortunate and not nearly as entertaining, I know, but simply a fact of life.

Thea went from throwing little scenarios my way to writing full-length scripts. Eddie's acting prowess progressed to the point that he was unafraid of any role. He could sink near-instantly into the character he needed to fill. Valerie went from debate team captain to class president as seamlessly as she made her arguments. Victor's blue streak returned to blonde hair, ending his goth phase, and bringing about a more mature side of him. He learned how to talk, not argue with Valerie and their relationship steadily went from volatile to reliable.

They all changed, upgraded even.

I, on the other hand, seemed to be unchanging. I remained as consistently boring as I had always been. It became what I was known for. I remained as uncomfortable being myself as I had always been, so I did my best to never be me and never being yourself doesn't allow for much development. I can't entirely blame my stagnant personality on how boring I truly am because, in that respect, it is partly my fault. When you spend years pretending to be anyone but yourself, whoever you were starts to fade out of existence. I did my best to fade into the background even when beneath the spotlight.

Now Thea's across the country, living it up in Los Angeles and writing plays at the University of Southern California. I remember the day she received her acceptance package (yes package) and how she called me in tears. All those years of decoding Valerie's choked-out sobs paid off because otherwise I would have had no idea what language she had been speaking, let alone what she was saying. Luckily for me, my parents were carpooling, so I drove right on over in my mom's less-than-lovely pale blue minivan, scooped her up, and took her out for celebratory coffees at the Roast.

That wasn't the only time we'd celebrated important life happens there. In fact, those old, upholstered cushions likely held more of our tears, happy and sad, than we could ever hope to produce in a single sitting. Home to the tears of years of break-ups, make-ups, break-downs, and build-ups, the Roast was not just a coffee shop, it was a house of memories, a home for troubled theatre kids.

Who would have thought the final member of our group would've come about thanks to that very day, in that very familiar place?

It was the day Thea told me of her directorial debut, of all her begging and pleading with Mitchell having finally paid off. In an email thread, dozens long, comprised entirely of her asking for a chance and asking again, the final message read Mitchell's well-thought-out response: "sure." Despite the situation's anticlimactic nature, Thea's joy told me that celebrations were indeed in order.

As I dragged Thea in through the single door to the chime of the bell strung above it, I noticed a change in surroundings. The Roast was supposed to be like me, unchanging. But something had changed.

Behind the counter, he fiddled with the machines and the different flavor syrups. It was clearly his first day because not only had I had never seen him before, but I had also never seen such a strong case of the first-day jitters.

For some reason, I didn't only see them, but I could feel them.

The change was unexpected and unnecessary. Some things can be perfect without change and the Roast was one of them. I am not. He was an unwelcome change of no fault of his own. I didn't want to hold it against him, so I went up to the register as I normally would. I had to clear my throat to get his attention.

"Oh, hi, sorry, what can I get you?" he asked after he quickly turned around to actually do his job.

He wasn't even wearing the visor correctly.

Everything about his existence in that very moment was wrong.

"Yeah, can I get one Stacey McHotness and one Volatile?" I asked, Thea, standing beside me still shaking from excitement.

A confused look crossed his face. He obviously hadn't been properly trained yet.

"Just two iced coffees, one with cream," I sighed. I'd really wanted my avocado mocha, but he was far too incompetent to make it.

"Alright, those I can do," he chuckled, "Got a name for the order?"

"Thea on the one with creamer and Jane on the other," I said dryly because even his laughter—however innocent it was—annoyed me.

"Alright, thanks Jane, I'll have these right out," he grinned.

I cocked an eyebrow, about to ask how he knew my name.

"You don't seem like the creamer type," he said as he scribbled onto the plastic cup.

I rolled my eyes and tugged Thea to the couch. As we sat down, she looked over at me, no longer shaking with excitement but instead bobbing back and forth with it. She was beaming at me.

"What?" I asked with a small chuckle.

"Oh me, oh my, my little Janey-Waney has grown up so fast!" she said, placing one arm to her forehead, her other hand clutching her chest, and flung her head back with her eyes closed, "What is a mother to do? My nest cannot be empty, not so soon!"

I couldn't help but laugh. And she said I was the dramatic one. "Thea, honey, I think the crying must've left you dehydrated. You sound absolutely insane. What are you rattling on about?" I asked, moving her arm aside so I could rest the back of my palm on her forehead. I was worried she'd gotten feverish.

"I think he's digging you," Thea said with a girlish smirk. It wasn't often we talked about boys so whenever even the slightest opportunity arose, she was overjoyed.

"Pfft," I blew a strand of my boring mud-colored hair out of my boring mud-colored eyes and crossing my arms, "There's not a chance in hell. Why would you even think that?"

"Oh c'mon, don't tell me you didn't notice him looking you up and down," she said.

I did, but I'd never admit that to her.

"He had a real case of the crushy-klutzies, my friend. It's obvious. What color flowers are you thinking for the wedding? Can I help pick the bridesmaids' dresses? Of course I can, I'll be the maid of honor, after all" Thea said with a cheeky grin.

I quickly covered her mouth, "Can you at least keep it down if you're going to babble like a lunatic?"

Being her, she licked my hand to free herself. Being me, I was appalled and quickly pulled my hand away, lunging instead for the nearest napkin. "How *dare* you," I huffed, rubbing her saliva off my skin. The feeling lingered, like a rash that wouldn't go away.

"Oh what, are you *embarrassed?*" she grinned, nudging my shoulder. "Ooh, look, here comes lover boy."

"Shut up," I nudged her back. I wasn't embarrassed because of what she was suggesting, I was embarrassed that he'd think I had that opinion of him when I was in fact indifferent. Well, actually, if I were to have any opinion of him, it would be a negative one. He was change and I didn't like it.

"Alright, one iced coffee with creamer for Thea," the barista boy said handing her the cup.

"Do you have a name? We're regulars here and we haven't seen you around before," Thea said, nudging his elbow in just the worst way humanly possible.

Before he could even process a response, I was covered in creamer-less iced coffee.

Thea gasped as I instinctually leaped up, knocking right into his chest.

The pure horror on his face was almost funny enough to make me forget that he'd just ruined my favorite tank top. "I—oh gosh, I'm so sorry, I'll go grab some napkins, I'm so so sorry," he said, scurrying to the nearest napkin dispenser.

"Just—I—" I stammered, so annoyed that I had lost the ability to speak.

He shuffled back over, an abundance of napkins in hand. As he reached out to wipe the coffee and chunks of ice clinging to my chest, I swatted his hand away and ripped the napkins. "I've got it," I snapped, "Go and get a mop or something…"

I paused for his name, simply because I wanted it to roll off my tongue and bound straight into his chest. I wanted my words to sting.

"Beckett," he said with a jolt as if startled by his own name.

"Yeah, whatever, go get a mop, *Bucket*," I snarled. It was a mediocrely clever jab at the time, but I had never anticipated it being a nickname I'd use to this day, a term of endearment in a way.

He, like any good little barista, scurried off to fetch a mop and his namesake while I was left with Thea's gawking gaze as I did what little I could do to clean myself up.

"Thanks a lot, T," I muttered, not mad about the boy or the coffee, no, just mad about the tank top and my once-white-now-light-brown sneakers.

"I'm sorry, Jane… Do you need more napkins? I can—" I cut her off.

"No, you've done enough," I huffed, shifting a glance to her moments later. She sat there, her head hanging with the weight of guilt, twiddling her thumbs like she always did when she wanted to do something, anything or say something, anything. I sighed. It was just a tank top. They were just shoes.

"It's alright, just a mistake. Typical T," I sat down and nudged her shoulder.

"Yeah, yeah," she smiled slightly and nudged mine back.

Beckett returned minutes later with a mop, a bucket, and a fresh iced coffee, holding it out to me. "I'm real sorry about that, miss. This one's on the house."

"Accidents happen," I shrugged, "I'm guessing especially often with someone as clumsy as you around, Bucket."

He laughed, a small, almost breathless kind of laugh, "Yeah, guess so."

I clicked my tongue, chuckling as I shook my head.

He was change, yes, but maybe change wasn't always *so* bad.

CHAPTER 2

Acting Out

Sometimes, looking back on it, I really should've done more in high school.

It's not like I wasn't involved, I just wasn't *involved*. Sure, I was in the drama club, but did I bother to learn everyone's names? No. Sure I went to pep rallies, but did I ever cheer or care or even attempt to look up from the phone screen that could've had its pixels sewn into my eyes? Never. I attended class, but would I have ever dreamed of raising my hand? Not a chance.

I just floated through four years of my life, at least that's how it's begun to feel when I stare up at the ceiling of my dorm, trying to block out whatever obscene sounds snake their way through the paper-thin walls. As a theatre major, you'd think I'd be used to the theatrics of whatever is occurring behind those walls but, in truth, it seems to have been a rather uncomfortable situation for us all.

But I wasn't a *true* theatre major. I almost wasn't even a theatre major at all. I was never even meant to appear on a stage. That was all Thea's doing, her influence on my life reaching a peak our sophomore year of high school.

~

Mr. Mitchell was anything but what a teacher should be.

When you said you wanted to do something, he didn't hold your hand, he flung you headfirst into the pit that you dug for yourself. When Thea told him she wanted to cast and direct and write, he took not just a single step but steps back and watched her fail.

"If you want to give up," he used to say, "Do it. Fling yourself on the ground and give up. You won't last very long. Wallowing in your self-pity puddle gets boring far too fast."

This phrase was so commonly thrown my way I may as well get it tattooed on my forehead. The longest I ever lasted in a state of giving up was about three hours.

Then, just as Mr. Mitchell predicted, I got bored.

I still remember the shock of hearing him tell me to give up for the first time. It wasn't that it wasn't something a teacher should be allowed to say, it's just something a teacher had never said before. There were plenty of times I wish a teacher had told me to give up.

In third grade, when I said I wanted to be a superhero and, rather than be told to give up, I was encouraged and told I could be whatever I wanted to be. That was a fun three-hour hospital visit of resetting the bones in my leg and stitching up the gash in my arm, side effects of my short and only attempt at flight. In middle school, when I wanted to be an edgy punk rock bassist, my music teacher told me to go for it. Meanwhile, I have a very large paperweight that looks strikingly like a bass guitar collecting dust in my room back home.

Mr. Mitchell wasn't the kind to toss encouragement your way.

He made you look for it, all on your own.

The first time he told me to give up was after I saw the casting calls for the production of Romeo and Juliet. Any normal actor would be ecstatic to receive a lead role.

I am no normal actor. I wasn't even an actor at this time, I hadn't yet joined the drama club. I was just a girl who liked to read lines for her friend, nothing more.

"No, no, this has to be some kind of mistake," I said, staring in horror and disbelief at that sheet of paper stapled to the wall, "I didn't even audition."

Juliet: Jane Carter

"No mistake, Miss Carter, you earned it," Mr. Mitchell said, patted my shoulder once, and arched a brow as to tell me to not make him regret it. But regret it he would.

⌇

That's right. I didn't audition, not formally at least. When I say Thea is smart, I mean she is the kind of smart you expect to take over the world one day, the kind of smart you worry about turning on you one day. She has always been maniacal, and she really outdid herself on that occasion.

It was a rainy Thursday afternoon and Thea had drama club. We'd walked home together every day for years until she joined the club, and I resented it for that. I hated walking home alone, especially in the rain, and Thea knew it.

I huffed heavily as I slammed my locker door shut, the damp air somehow having slipped through the cracks of my school to frizz up my hair because of course it had. As I blew a clump of frizzed-up-boring-brown hair out of my eyes, Thea pressed her back to the locker beside me, her forearm rested dramatically on her forehead—a signature move of hers really—as she sunk down to the floor.

"Oh, my poor Janey-Waney! Frizzed up hair and a frown falling harder than the rain! Whatever will she do?" Thea asked God perhaps. I couldn't tell who she was talking to.

"Oh, hush up. If you hadn't ditched me for drama club, I wouldn't be stuck in the rain alone. At least I'd have company," I said, stuffing my books into my satchel. I'd always preferred them to backpacks when it came to carrying school supplies and textbooks.

"Why not find company…with *the* company!" she sprung up, a bright grin on her lips almost powerful enough to break through the barricade of grey clouds that hung in the sky.

"Huh?" I arched a brow, mostly because I had no idea what company she was talking about.

"Come to drama club with me! It'll be fun," she drew out her words, "There'll be cute boys. And only half of them are gay."

"Oh, I don't know about that. I don't think I'd really fit in…" I ran my fingers through frizzed out ends, knowing I meant to say something more along the lines of "me not fitting in would be a fact, not a thought to consider."

"But you'll get to spend more time with me! How could you possibly say no?" Thea pouted, crossing her arms, dramatic as always.

"Maybe another time T, I should probably get goi—" I paused at the clap of thunder and the flash of lightning, "Y'know on second thought maybe avoiding this rain isn't the worst idea in the world."

"Thank you, mother nature!" Thea grinned, grabbed my arms, and dragged me off. For a 5'3 writing nerd, she really could tug me around like a ragdoll whenever she felt like it. Not like I'd fight it, anyway.

Before I even had the time to realize it, I was standing in front of a glorious, raised stage. The chatter of actors rung in my ears. Costumes flew person to person. Sewing kits, makeup bags, and props of all sorts scattered across the seats. The lights came and went like the lightning outside, but with more control, and much more dictation. To think that all of this could come together into one cohesive set of two hours was mind-boggling. But eventually, that chaos became second nature, a sort of homeostatic state in which I lived and, dare I say, thrived. Or at least it was a state in which I used to live, used to thrive, not now that everything is so boring.

"Welcome to a lovely storm!" Thea beamed with widespread arms, taking a large step onto the stage, and then aimed two finger guns my way, "And, if you play your cards right, you can stick around."

I snapped out of my dazed amazement. "Whoa, whoa, whoa, slow down…"

She cut me off, "Don't worry, I know the chances of getting you up here are slim to none but maybe you could do crew? Or tech? That way we could go back to walking home together. What do you think?" Her eyes were pleading.

"Oh, I dunno T… Maybe, I'll think about it," I conceded.

"That's all I ask!" she grinned, throwing her arms into the air, and doing a quick spin on the tips of her toes. It's only now I see she'd been lying through her teeth. They always say hindsight is 20/20, after all. I certainly didn't have the foresight to see through her little game. She played me like a violin and dammit, she was a prodigy.

"C'mon, I'll show you around," she bounced as she spoke. She dragged me behind stage to show me all the actors prepping lines.

"Why does everyone look so stressed?" I asked, tilting my head at the boisterous looking redhead who'd been applying white face paint and eyeliner.

"It's audition day, silly. Everyone wants a lead. I mean, c'mon, who wouldn't? We're putting on *Romeo and Juliet*, after all! Ugh, a classic! No self-respecting theatre company would dare screw it up! We have to find just the right people for the parts, or everything will just fall apart," she rattled on as she tugged me even further to the dressing rooms and costume racks. I couldn't help but be amazed at this organized mess.

"How do you guys find anything in here?" I asked, imagining the fit my mom would have if my room looked even remotely like this. She likely would've asked if I had been raised in a barn and if she had failed me as a mother. Neither of which were true but both of which she would have the right to assume.

"Oh, you really get used to it after a while. There is a system, I swear. You just don't know it," Thea said, and then added, "yet." Before I could get a chance to protest, we were off again.

"And this," Thea said, pulling open the door to a cramped office as if it were the door to a palace, "is where I get my work done." She beamed as she waved a hand around the place. A desk, a creaky looking office chair, and a typewriter were all that occupied it aside from us. The walls were blank and windowless, without a motivational cat poster in sight.

"How could you possibly get any work done in here? It's so boring," I said and quickly bit my tongue because, even in that moment, I realized how rude a thing that was to say. She seemed so excited to show me this space and I bashed it. But her grin only grew wider.

"Exactly! No windows, no pictures, no Wi-Fi, no computer, nothing to distract me," she said, "It's really spiked my productivity. Look." She held out a large stack of typewritten papers to me. Even they felt boring and outdated, yet the words on them were anything but.

"A scene?" I asked.

Thea shook her head, "A script."

I arched a brow, astonished. Up to that point, she'd only ever written one-shots of minor significance. A whole script, even I didn't think she had it in her.

"Well, c'mon then. Do your thing," Thea said after a few moments of waiting, swaying from heel to toe, expecting me to jump into character the second she put the stack of papers in my hands as I always did but this wasn't the Roast. This wasn't familiar, it was change and it was uncomfortable.

"Oh, I 'dunno, T, maybe some other time…" I mumbled. She could tell I was clamming up. She always could.

"Please," she drew out the word for a good ten seconds, only to end up sputtering out, "I haven't shown this to anyone else and I've worked so hard on it, and I can't imagine anyone but you being the first person to give it a go and if you don't, I think I'll die, watch, I'll die, I'll do it right here."

I sighed heavily to cut her off. "Okay, okay, will you shut your yap already? I can't get in character if you just start dying on me, now, can I?"

The sound that escaped her lips was a cross between a squeal, a shriek, and a gasp as she leapt into her chair, spun in a full circle, and rested her chin on her clasped fingers. "Okay. I'm ready," she said once she had fully composed herself and taken a nice deep breath, as if she was the one who needed to get into character, "Whenever you are, that is." She did her best to appear patient but, while she was as dramatic and theatrical as anyone there, she couldn't act. At least, I thought she couldn't. I guess everyone plays a part —whether onstage or off.

And so, I slipped away, into the head of another, and for a moment I was someone better than I could ever be. I couldn't tell you what the lines I read had been, but I can tell you that in that moment, I felt as free as I have ever felt, as whole as I have ever felt, and as me as I could ever feel. Thea sat there silently and let me play with the notion of what I could be, using her words as a vessel. She didn't say a word or make a sound; she scarcely breathed. It was only after I set her script down on and bowed and clapped and, not to my knowledge at the time, someone else had done so silently as well.

Mr. Mitchell reminded me nearly every day of what a wonderful audition I gave, even if it was given against my will.

Thea: 1 Jane: 0

She told him to be there, to listen in on my little performance and said that if he did so, he wouldn't be disappointed.

He wasn't.

The disappointment I was sure to bring came much, much later.

***

She tricked me into coming again that next week. She "forgot her umbrella" at home and needed to borrow mine. She was prone to catching colds and, even if the rain really has nothing to do with it, she insisted upon borrowing mine. At first, I refused but she promised me a coffee that next morning and, with a caffeine addiction like mine, just like that she'd suckered me in. Playing both the guilt trip and the addiction cards was a bold move on her part, I figured she must have really been desperate.

"Jane!" Thea ran over to the door as I stepped in, taking the umbrella from my hands only to take my hands and tug me inside. "It's too cold out there, come warm up inside, okay? I can't have you catching a cold because of such a noble sacrifice."

"Nothing noble about it, I expect that coffee tomorrow," I chuckled, shoving my hands in my pockets. I knew I couldn't argue with her or slip away, and she was right, it was rather cold. I figured there was no harm in warming up before heading out.

I never got to head out.

She slowly guided me over to the sheet of paper that sealed my fate. I should've guessed something was up by all the dirty looks I got when she called out my name. They all knew something I didn't; they all knew I stole something they believed belonged to them. Thea knew better than to stick around after I saw my name on that single sheet tombstone. When I turned around, she'd vanished, slithered away into her little writing den to hide from my fury.

I wasn't as mad as I should've been. She'd played me like a game, and it took me far too long to put the pieces together, so the blame was partly mine. I was frozen not in rage, but in shock, in fear.

I stood there for what could've been hours, gazing at my name printed in black ink on white paper. It seemed too good to be true and too bad to be false. He couldn't possibly expect me to get on a stage after hearing me read a couple lines in some janitor's closet of an office just one time, could he? Of course, he could, he was the theatre teacher. They were always allowed to be weird and make seemingly certifiable choices.

Once everyone had left, either bearing faces of excitement, disappointment, or the occasional occurrence of rage, I sank to my knees in disbelief. Why me? Only I could've possibly ended up getting cast in a play I didn't even audition for.

All I could think about was how there was no way in hell that I could do this and how Thea was definitely going to hear about it once she slithered out of her locked little writing closet like the snake she was. I had never expected such deceit, such betrayal, and albeit such cunning from her. It was terrifying, hurtful, and impressive all at once. Could I really be upset at that great a plan? In that moment I wasn't quite sure what I felt other than a dull ache in my knees from the hardwood floor.

"Juliet, Juliet, why fore art thou on thine knees? Unless it beeth me you wish to please," I heard a voice chime from behind me, pulling me out of my thoughts and nearly pulling my lunch from my stomach with the vulgarity of the comment. I glanced back, staring incredulously at the redheaded boy. As I stood, I drew a hand back and slapped him. He deserved it. Maybe, in reality, he didn't, but in the fictional space I was being pulled into, he did.

"Ow, what was that for?" he asked, grabbed my wrist in one hand before I could backhand him while the other rubbed his cheek.

"I didn't like your tone," I chose my words carefully, my gaze drifting from the handprint on his cheek to the redness of my palm. I think he picked up on the mood and my shell-shocked state pretty fast because his retaliation for my physical assault never came.

"Okay, alright, fair enough. I'm sorry, I was just trying to get into character. You're the Juliet to my Romeo after all," he grinned as he released my hand and dropped his to his side. I arched a brow at him, smirking slightly at the red imprint of my palm on his cheek contouring to contain his smile, before glancing back at the casting call.

Romeo: Edison Bishop

"I'm Edison. But I'd prefer if you'd call me Eddie." He ran a hand through his fiery curls and made a half-bow.

"Alright, Eddie, well, I hate to break it to you, but I don't plan on being your Juliet for much longer. Mr. Mitchell made a mistake," I said, blowing a strand of hair away from my eyes.

"Did he? I haven't known Mitchell to make mistakes. Ever. And I've been doing shows with him since I was a kid," Edison said with a near hint of pride. I also noticed he dropped the Mr. from Mitchell's title. I took note of that familiarity as if it was information somehow, I knew I needed. What's strange is that even at that moment, I wasn't planning on staying long. Perhaps in my heart, I knew I wasn't going anywhere.

"Since you were a kid, huh? Well, I hate to shatter your grandiose childhood image of the man, but he made a mistake, *I* am a mistake. I didn't audition. I shouldn't even be here," I said as I attempted to make my way to the director's office.

Edison grabbed my wrist. "Hey, whoa, no. He put you in the lead role for a reason. Oh! Y'know what, I have just the thing for cold feet, c'mon!" And just like that, I was being dragged around once again, this time to the men's dressing room.

"I don't really think I should be in here," I said, awkwardly looking around. Though, it's not like it made much of a difference. The men's and women's dressing rooms were the same, except one was amess with scattered clothing and one was amess with empty makeup bottles, though which was which could change depending on the day and show.

"Oh please, we're all actors here. You're not really friends with someone until you help them get into costume, after all," Edison said, only releasing my wrist to dig to the bottom of what seemed to be a bin of hats.

"What are you looking for?" I arched a brow, wondering how he could be looking for anything at all in that mess.

"You'll see soon enough, aha!" he triumphantly held a freezer-sized Ziplock bag above his head with the same pride of a warrior hoisting up his slain enemy's remains.

"Are those…cupcakes?"

He gasped, his free hand clutching his chest with the same air of offense he'd have had I called his grandmother a Capulet.

"How *dare* you! These are no mere cupcakes. Cupcakes are juvenile. These, my friend, are Ding Dongs, only the finest snack cake Hostess produces." I was beginning to understand why Thea felt so at home with them.

"What in the world is a Ding Dong?" I couldn't help but laugh at his absurd passion for something so unimportant. Cupcake, Ding Dong, snack cake, they were all essentially the same thing. I didn't get what the big deal was.

"You…how could you…this must be rectified!" he shouted at the top of his lungs and tossed a Ding Dong my way with the power of an all-star pitcher.

"Whoa!" I gasped as I caught it, barely avoiding a snack-cake-induced black eye, the inevitable nickname that followed such an event, and the ensuing embarrassing story that I'd be forced to tell my children someday. I know it sounds ridiculous, but with the strength behind his throw, I felt my life flash before my eyes. It was just as boring as I imagined.

"Eat it. Right now. There's no time to waste. You've been living in the dark ages for far too long, I'm here to offer you salvation and salivation!"

As I opened the clear, crinkly packaging, all I could think about was what a character he was. He watched me carefully, longing clawing out of his eyes. "Why don't you eat one with me?"

"Oh, I will, trust me, I just need to be wholly present to experience this moment with you," he took a deep breath and raised his clasped hands to his lips as I took my first bite. And, to tell you the truth, it tasted just like a Hostess Cupcake but there was no way in hell I was going to tell him that.

"So?" he asked, drawing out his words.

"This…is incredible!" I cried. In that moment, I thought perhaps Mr. Mitchell was right. Maybe I was fit for the stage. Convincing Eddie was a piece of cake, after all. Maybe I did have it in me. But don't think I'd changed my mind about marching right into his office and quitting the show. I needed a lot more to change my mind and I'd get it.

"Well, are you feeling a little better about all of this? Being a lead and all?" Eddie arched a brow, leaning his back against the wall as he takes a bite of an unwrapped Ding Dong.

"Not in the slightest. Though, I do feel a bit more satiated," I said, tossing the wrapper in a trash can.

"Huh?" This is where I took note and planned to get Eddie a dictionary.

"Less hungry, more full," I chuckled and shook my head, walking towards the door.

"Whoa, where do you think you're going?" he asked, grabbing my arm again, "Well, I mean, you're free to leave but not if you're going to tell Mitchell that you're not fit to be a lead. Just give it a chance, alright? Give yourself a chance."

"I never planned on giving myself a chance in the first place, so why start now?" I shrugged his arm away and tried to leave. He was very insistent and kept pulling me back, either with his hand or his words.

"Okay, okay, listen, let me try one more thing, yeah? And if you still want to quit, you can, and I won't stand in your way. Deal?"

I hesitated but, genuinely curious. I obliged and shook his hand, "Deal."

And with that, he dragged me outside.

"Whoa, it's raining, don't we need an umbrella?!"

"Nope!" he grinned defiantly, and we plunged out into the rain, "C'mon then, catch up!" Almost in the blink of an eye, he took off sprinting and I was left behind to watch the puddles leap up beneath his feet.

"What?!" I chuckled and, after a moment of foolishly standing and watching, I took off after him. He led me around the entire school. We ran across every sports field and leapt over the outdoor dining commons. Well, he leapt, I stumbled and occasionally fell. Only later did I learn he was a hurdler on the track and field team. Dirty cheater.

He eventually came to a startlingly harsh stop, causing me to slam right into his back. I, unlike him, couldn't end my full-on sprint nearly as well as he could.

He caught me, wrapping an arm around my waist, "Whoa there, don't go falling for me quite yet. Save that for the stage, alright Juliet?"

"Hey now, nobody said I'd agreed, clue me into why you brought me out here and why we're freezing our asses off," I said and took a step away.

"Isn't it obvious? Look around you," he motioned to the empty field surrounding us.

I didn't get it. He caught onto my confusion yet offered me no explanation. He only took a seat on the wet grass and opened his mouth not to speak, but to scream.

"What? What are you doing?" I asked, astonished, but he didn't answer. He just sat on the soaking wet grass in his sopping wet clothes and screamed his heart out. The only word I could use to describe that moment is glorious. I didn't get it at first but then it clicked.

He was untying his balloon.

A strange notion, I know, but it's something my dad always told me to do back in my overwhelmingly angsty years. He didn't like the cliché of a bottle. He thought of people as flexible things, hard to know the limit of until it was already reached.

"There's a lot going on right now, I know," he'd say, "Your body's changing…"

That's where I'd cut him off to gag.

"And your mind is all jumbled up. You don't know who you are or who you're going to be. You don't know what you want to do with your life quite yet and that's okay. Hell, I psychoanalyze parakeets for a living. There's just so much you don't know yet. And with people on top of that, oh gosh, people are a drag. Sometimes animals are easier to understand. Not even sometimes, a lot of the time it's easier to get a dog to let me in than to get you to."

He'd nudge my side and ruffle my hair. Depending on my mood I'd roll my eyes and nudge him back or groan and not listen to the rest of his speech.

"You're finding your way in the world, and I get that. I was there once. But you've gotta let it out sometimes, kiddo. The cat can't have your tongue all the time. Think of yourself like a balloon," he'd make a vaguely balloon-like shape with his hands.

"You can take in a lot, y'know? The mind can handle a lot of stress, like a balloon with air, and a little stress is good. You don't want to get too comfortable, just like a balloon shouldn't be flat.

But too much stress…too much air…" He'd make a popping noise with one of his fingers and the inside of his cheek. "And you'll burst, just like a balloon. Sometimes you have to untie your balloon. It doesn't have to be to me, or to anyone for that matter, but you've got to untie it sometimes. I can't have my baby balloon popping on me." He'd ruffle my hair again.

Regardless of my mood, this is where I would just groan and leave, likely more annoyed than I had been to begin with because somewhere deep down inside me I knew he was right. Only now am I able to say that out loud.

But that's exactly what Eddie was doing, in a picturesque way might I add. With water droplets dripping from his fiery curls and his lips blue and his nose red, Eddie was in the rain, screaming like a madman, untying some imaginary balloon filled with stress and worry and doubt. Somehow, someway, he knew that was exactly what I needed. I hated that Eddie was like my father in that way. From the moment he met my kneeling form, he knew exactly what I needed even if I didn't, even if I didn't want what I needed.

He was my alarm clock when my dreams were too unruly, my wake-up call.

I hesitated, but I really shouldn't have. I knew I wanted to sit there in the pouring rain and belt my heart out to the silver sky, scream until each raindrop held my pitch and, plopping into puddles, imitated it. But instead, I hesitated, stood there watching him for a few more wonderful moments before I, for the second time that day, sunk to my knees.

The only differences were that this time, I was screaming, and, this time, I had someone by my side.

CHAPTER 3

Moving Forward

Hardly over a month into the semester and midterms have already hit me like a truck. No, something worse. A train maybe? With a medium amount of cars. Not so long that it seems like there's no end in sight, but just long enough so that you can see the second, poorly scheduled train called "finals" approaching.

Regardless, midterms have been ruthless. Like a blitz, they have been coming in waves, one right after the other with barely any time to breathe in between.

This moment, for me at least, is an inhale. An exhale will be soon to come, and strangulation via statistics and geology will take me to my knees, but for now, I can breathe.

You would think that I'd care enough to take notes in geology as my professor droned on and on, projecting so much as to soak his mustache in spit, because another midterm was fast approaching, but sadly my mind refused to work in such a logical way. Instead, I was slumped over my notebook, nearly drooling onto the page, and sketching. Sometimes I did it just to put my thoughts down, as insignificant as they were.

Doodles of my professor's drenched mustachioed face, of my dream flying minivan, of a volcano that spewed molten nacho cheese, left my paper covered in graphite and eraser shavings. Not exactly a worthwhile use of my time, but one that kept my mind busy. And off of how hungry I was, in case you were wondering what the volcano was about.

I've always had a bad habit of doodling instead of taking notes and the habit wasn't going away anytime soon from what I could tell.

There were few times when this so-called skill ever came in handy but those that did were lifesaving. A bit of an exaggeration, yes, but a wholehearted one. One such instance came to mind as I drifted into that sweet state of daydreams, my mind flooded back to simpler times, younger years, happier days.

⁓⁓⁓

"Wow, look at that, our little Juliet isn't just a talented actress, she's an artist as well," I heard a voice, no, it was two in harmony, chime over my shoulder in my high school economics class. And, before your judgment shoots at me like bullets, ask yourself if you could keep your mind from straying in a high school economics course. Yeah, that's what I thought.

Typically, I didn't care if someone saw my stupid little sketches but, for some reason, my cheeks flushed at the word Juliet. Perhaps I had yet to accept that I had not awakened from my nightmare of a casting call. I pulled my notebook to my chest and held it close, clutching it with lead-weighted arms. My whole body felt stiff and heavy and hot like a molten fluid poured into my veins only to cool and harden, leaving me a statue.

"Maybe you could mind your own business. And I'm nobody's Juliet," I said as I turned my head, notebook still in arms like a shield guarding my racing heart. I felt as if I'd been caught with red hands, but my hands were white and clammy, all my blood rushed to add color to my face. Why did I care so much?

"Hey now, no need to get snappy with us. We're only admiring," Valerie grinned. I should have known it was Vic and Val, only they could've spoke so in unison.

"No need to get embarrassed," Victor patted my shoulder, leaving a bit of black residue on my t-shirt from when he undoubtedly touched up his guy-liner. As scary as he looked, Vic was a nice guy with a good heart. He had a lot of compassion underneath his fake blood-splattered hoodie and spiked leather belt.

"C'mon, we already got a peek, you may as well let us see," Valerie pleaded.

It had been a week since their first break-up debacle. Meaning it had been a week since we'd started rehearsals. Mr. Mitchell asked me if I wanted to wear a corset in the show to make everything seem more authentic and Thea jumped in saying that if I didn't it'd be a travesty, an utter disappointment to the time period we were trying to capture on our stage. Her use of the words 'we' and 'our' annoyed me because I had never made the choice to become a part of this little world of hers but there I was, forced onto the stage to begin with and then forced into a corset. All I could do was sigh and say sure, why not.

I rehearsed wearing it every single time. Why you wonder? Because otherwise, I wouldn't be capable of wearing it on stage for so long. I had to train my body for it, at least that's what Thea said. And I hated every moment of that damned contraption.

"Thea, I swear if you don't get this thing off me, I'm going to chew through it," I muttered, clutching the counter in the women's dressing room as she tried and failed again and again to untie the strings that pushed my organs into my throat.

"Look, it's not my fault you went and knotted the strings!" Thea said, struggling with the tangled torture web until she staggered back. "This thing just won't budge."

"That's just cause you're not putting your back into it. I already have my back in it so stop standing around and get me out of this thing already. It's your fault I'm stuck wearing it anyway!" I snapped, "Oh, you know what? I have an idea! How about we just cut it off!"

"No way in hell! Do you have any idea how expensive that is? You can't just cut it off!" she cried.

"Then hurry up and get it untied already," I said, and she went back to struggling with the strings. It was so tight I could barely even expand my lungs enough to suck in a breath, but it was the aesthetic she was looking for, so my feelings were pushed aside when it came to the matter, just as they were with any other matter. The show had to be perfect, after all, even if there was an unwilling, unwitting participant.

"I think I…almost…got it!" she said, and the strings fell to my side and the corset slipped down to my ankles. I wrapped my arms around me, shielding myself the eyes that enter cramped dressing rooms, and, as if I'd had a premonition, the door burst wide open, and a girl's sobs echoed through the room.

The girl slammed the door behind her and leaned against it. She wiped her mascara-smudged eyes with hands that looked like baby penguin's pulled from an oil spill. She paid little heed to my flushed visage and exposed frame. Instead, in one burst of breath, she got out what I assume were words as half of what she said was unintelligible at best. The most I managed to get out of it was "Victor…he's such a…I can't believe…pain in my…heart" and then the second bit of dialogue, much more comprehensible, "What am I going to do?"

I couldn't help but feel a bit relieved because at least I had gone from *the* most ridiculous looking person in the room to the *second* most ridiculous looking person in the room. Thea, after recovering from the shock of it all, regained her common sense and quickly tossed me her hoodie, which I immediately pulled on and only then turned to the girl.

"It's alright, go ahead and cry it out Val, I'm sure this is all his fault, we're here for you," she said and placed a hand on her shoulder to console her.

The girl wiped her eyes again and glanced up at me as I covered myself and clumsily tossed the corset, which up until then had hung around my ankles, aside. "What the hell were you two even doing in here…?" she half-laughed, half-sniffled. The more I think about it, the stranger the situation must've seemed to her, especially since it was super early-on in rehearsals, and I was the only one forced to be somewhat in costume.

"Look, it wasn't anything weird, okay?" I piped up, still rather flustered from being half-naked in front of my best friend *and* a total stranger.

"You're right, you're right, it's none of my business anyway. We're an inclusive club here so there's no need to be shy," she said, sniffling less and laughing more this time.

My face burned even hotter when Thea joined in. I hadn't quite gotten used to the humor of the bunch so the whole "shipping" thing was lost on me. Soon enough it was second nature, but I can still feel my eyelashes singing at the heat of my burning coals for cheeks. "Hey now, don't go getting jealous, Valerie. You had your chance, but you chose Victor," Thea nudged her side.

"Ah, I know, what a fool I was! And here you go and snag yourself a pretty thing like her. What a grave mistake I've made," Valerie rolled her eyes, enunciating her words like Thea did when she was trying to be as dramatic as possible.

She shifted her glance towards me and held out one of her oil-spill victim hands. "Don't be too embarrassed. Everyone gets a peek at each other eventually. And you have nothing to worry about," she chuckled when I tomatoed once again as I took her hand, "What's your name newbie?"

"Jane, uh, Jane Carter," I said, stumbling over my words as my pulse slowed to its normal, average pace.

"You sure about that, cause you don't sound—hey wait, are you telling me you're our Juliet?" she gasped and looked over at Thea, who nodded like an overly proud soccer mom who was watching their kid get handed a participation trophy for the fifth year in a row.

"No way! You're the one everyone's been talking about! From what I've heard you've got real talent, girly. I haven't gotten the chance to see you in action myself, too busy and all," she motioned down to herself. My eyes trailed up from her chimneysweep hand to her mosaic-like arms and her Pollock-esque shirt.

"Val here's our head set designer. She puts in more work than anyone to make sure we've got a setting so real our audience is whisked away," Thea grinned and wrapped an arm around her shoulders.

"Huh, couldn't tell," I said and cracked a small, I'm assuming awkward, smile. They both laughed, and I sighed in relief.

"Anyway, sorry we had to meet each other when we were both so…vulnerable," Valerie laughed and dried her eyes once again. I shook my head and laughed slightly, telling her it was fine.

"Look, T, I was hoping you could …" she began but Thea cut her off. I was glad to know I wasn't the only person she did that to.

"Work my magic and figure out what's making Vic such a dick? On it. You coming, Jane?" she turned to me.

"What? I'm not sure I'm all that qualified to intervene…" I said but she grabbed onto my arms and dragged me out of the dressing room anyway.

"Nonsense, no experience needed! And if there was, there's no way to get any without dealing with it firsthand! Let's go!" Thea marched on. I glanced back and watched Valerie close the door, inky tears already rolling down her cheeks again. Sometimes I wonder if she really wanted us to go find Victor, or if she just wanted a quiet place to be alone.

But find Victor we did. And oh boy was I not expecting what we found.

～

I'd seen this guy around campus before, he certainly was hard to miss. He was one of the only guys with colored hair, and the only one with an electric blue streak, that's for sure. Whenever I saw him, I thought he looked like the punk bully, not to be confused with the jock bully, in every 90's flick I'd ever seen. His style alternated from punk to emo, leather jacket to hoodies, but around campus, he always wore the same scowl regardless of how he was dressed or who he was talking to. I'd always thought to stay away from guys like him because they'd likely be trouble but, as I saw him sitting on the steps of the theatre, his guyliner dripping down his face and making smudges that matched Valerie's on his hands, I wondered how bad this guy could truly be.

Thea held none of my sympathy. She made that known in an instant.

"Well, well, well, Vic the dick strikes again. What'd you do this time? And don't try and blame it on Val, we both know it was all you. It always is," she plopped down on the steps next to him and punched his shoulder a little harder than she should've, making her presence known.

"Look, I don't need a lecture right now, okay?" he muttered, tugging closed the strings of his hoodie to hide his face in shame. He stuffed his hands away in his pockets and turned even further from her, hiding like a turtle in its shell.

Thea looked at me expectantly. I wasn't sure what exactly she wanted me to say, I didn't even know the guy.

"Well, um, Victor…" I spoke up, "Valerie seems really torn up about whatever happened between you two. Maybe you should go and talk to her? You seem pretty upset as well, maybe you can work things out?"

"Who even are you? You don't know anything about me and Val, so butt out," he muttered.

Yeah, what a nice guy, I thought.

"Hey now, chill out Vic, I know you're mad but that's no way to talk to our lead, let alone my best friend. Why don't you tell us what happened? Val didn't really tell us much," Thea jumped in to save the day.

The ball of darkness sitting on the steps sighed and sat up, wiping his eyes on the sleeves of his hoodie. "I told Val we should end things… for her sake."

"What do you mean for her sake?" Thea asked with an arched brow.

"Look, there's no easy way to say it but…I'm moving." he shrunk away once more.

"What? No way, you can't be serious," Thea raised her hands to her mouth as she gasped, genuinely shocked, "Where? When? Why?"

"I don't know, okay?" Victor snapped, then took a moment to compose himself, "My parents went to one of my dad's work's stupid fancy banquets and the phone in his office was ringing so I picked it up. It was some real-estate agent saying the sale went through and the property was sold. My dad's an investment banker so what kind of property would he be selling except our house? He's been saying he hates our house after all, and his boss came over for dinner and was talking about a new position in Maine. Maine, of all places."

"Okay, okay, that sounds bad but maybe you're reading too far into things? Maybe none of them have to do with each other?" Thea said, trying to sound hopeful while she looked fairly hopeless.

"Well, if I'm not right, why'd he text me saying he and my mom have some important news to tell me after I get home? What else could this news be?" Victor held his head in his hands, "I didn't want to hurt her, I just figure it was for the best to get it out of the way now."

"Y'know what? No, this isn't going to work. This program can't lose you and if we are going to lose you, we need to know now. Victor, go home right now and talk to your parents. We need to know what's going on. Jane, you go with Victor and bring him back to the Roast in an hour. I'm going to find Valerie and somehow convince her to get coffee with me. We'll reconvene there, with all the information, and work this shit out. Okay, go team!"

"But why do I have to go?" I said, but she had already run too far away to hear me, "with him…" I sighed heavily and offered my hand to Victor. "Well, you heard her."

He arched a brow then took my hand and stood up, "You don't seem so happy with your role in all of this…" He paused, waiting for me to introduce myself.

"Jane," I said and shrugged, "And it's a little strange, especially considering we've just met, but Thea's plans usually work out alright, so I may as well go with it."

He laughed slightly, wiping eyeliner tears away with his sleeves before beckoning me after him, "You're not wrong there. Thea's plans—however convoluted—always find their way of working themselves out."

We walked mostly in silence to his house. It didn't look like the house of an investment banker, or at least what I imagined the house of an investment banker to look like. Maybe instead the house of a small, quaint, perhaps a little odd, family instead. It was a pale shade of yellow, perhaps a tenth as vibrant as a Starburst, with a slate roof and a bay window right in the front. The steps leading up to the deck creaked and the wood of the overhang looked ready to rot away.

Certainly not the house I expected. I could see why his father was less than fond of it. Victor chuckled when he noticed me looking it over, "Not a fan?"

"No, no, it's…nice," I said, rubbing the back of my neck.

"You don't have to lie; I know it's a weird-looking place. I wouldn't like it either if I hadn't grown up here. I'll go inside and talk to them. You wait out here, okay?" he said.

"Uh, yeah, sure," I said as he went inside. My gaze drifted to a charming old bench swing. Against my better judgment, I took a seat. I sat for what felt like ages, wishing I had had the sense to bring my phone. When Victor eventually stepped outside, he looked like he'd seen a ghost. He took a seat beside me.

"Well?" I asked after a few moments of silence.

"We are moving…but not to Maine, to the next street over…" he said in a hushed tone.

I couldn't help but laugh at the absurdity of it all, "What? Why? Why go through all the trouble of moving if you're only going to the next street?"

"I'm going to be a big brother," Victor glanced at me, paler than any white face paint could've made him, "We need more space because my mom is pregnant."

Marvelous with words as ever, I mustered only a "Holy shit," in that beautiful moment.

"I," He said, running his hands through his hair and leaning back against the swing. Apparently this news conflicted him. "I'm going to be a brother, can you believe that?" he laughed, "Me, influencing a baby for the next few years. I guess my parents really couldn't deal with the fact that I'm already in high school, so they decided to start over. Can you believe that? Pregnant, all over again." He was grinning ear to ear and now the tears that rolled down his cheeks were happy ones. "I guess the curse of being the only child can only last for so long sometimes, huh Jane?" Victor glanced over at me.

"Wouldn't know, I never dealt with the curse all that long anyway." I smiled gently at him, placing my hand on his shoulder, "Congrats, Victor." What a way with words I had.

"A big brother, me? I can hardly keep myself in check, how am I going to look after a baby and make sure it doesn't end up as stupid as me?" he asked, more directed towards the setting sun than anyone else. He took a few moments to pull himself together before standing up and tugging me up with him, "C'mon then, there's no point in trying to figure all of this out now, that can wait. We have a coffee date to make. I've got to make things right."

And so, I got Victor to the Roast, where Thea had managed to drag Valerie, and everything sorted itself out. Victor told her everything: why he broke up with her, what his reasoning was, what the truth was, and how sorry he was.

She told him how stupid he was. Ruthless, but fair in my opinion.

Thea and I were decent enough to give them their space but not quite decent enough to forego eavesdropping. Thea justified it by saying she was always in need of inspiration for her next play, and I had nothing better to do as my phone was in the dressing room, left lying there alongside my shirt and my dignity.

To think that tangled mess of a day began with something as simple as a tangled mess. Funny how life works that way.

The next day was simpler yet shared many traits of the one before. I was bored in class and my attention fled my mind and sought shelter in the graphite tip of my pencil. Vic and Val sauntered up at the end to wake me from my stupor and pester me once more.

"C'mon then, Jane, it's not like you've got much left to hide from me," Valerie nudged my shoulder. I sighed and slid over my notebook, resigned to the fate that I'd have to share myself with these people.

"Seems like you've got nothing to lose," Victor chuckled, as he'd already heard the tale of our fateful acquaintance.

The drawings that day were less random than usual. A few coffee cups at a familiar table, a couple tilted on their sides, a few empty mugs flipped over to drip remnants of lattes out onto napkins. A bench swing on a deck, a bay window at its side, one sun setting in the distance while another one rose. A corset with a big red X crossing it out. And the best of them all, the most carefully drawn, two black-smudged hands clasping one another.

They didn't even mention that one though. They were too busy looking at the others to notice themselves on a page.

"Wow Jane, is that my house?" Victor asked, pointing to the sunset sketch.

I shrugged a shoulder. It was…but I figured perhaps it would've been weird to admit that I'd drawn his house.

"These are really good. How come you don't help me paint sets?" Valerie nudged me once again.

"It's nothing like that. These are just…" I hesitated.

"Just?" she arched a brow, curious.

"They're nothing more than pointless doodles. Just because I can do junk like this doesn't mean I could do a full blow set as you do. Leave the real work to the professionals, you know?" I glanced over at her.

"Oh, come on, I'm sure you could. I'm sure if I got a paintbrush in that hand of yours, you'd be a natural," Valerie grinned, "What's so different about doodles and sets?"

"Oh, I dunno, I can't really explain it," I shrugged once more. "People aren't even meant to see the former. If you two hadn't been so nosy I wouldn't have to explain the difference in the first place."

"Alright, alright, fine," Valerie chuckled and set my notebook back down in front of me, "You've got us there."

"Well, you've got more than one talent it seems," Victor ruffled my hair as the bell rang. "Catch you after school."

"See you later, Jane," Valerie waved and the two of them were off.

I sighed, flipping my notebook closed and stuffing it into my backpack. I thought about tearing that page out and throwing it away. Crumpling it up and tossing it out of my life, but that would've been entirely against the point.

You see, I don't think I doodled because I was bored that day. I think I did because I wanted to remember *that* day as vividly as it occurred, black smudged skin, sunset-filled shifting slowly to star-dappled sky, red flushed cheeks, and all.

CHAPTER 4

Missing Pieces

Getting grades back on my first round of midterms reminds me of a valuable lesson: the lesson of failure. One that I, personally, was lucky enough to have already received but I guess my professors didn't get the memo. I suppose it must not be a prerequisite or something they put on your transcript. No, it's just the topic of every single essay you write to get into the goddamn place, but I guess somewhere along the line they decided that I didn't learn it hard enough so here I am.

I may as well be registered for remedial failure. It's a class I've taken repeatedly and somehow never seem to pass, or at least get past.

But instead, I'm holed up in my room wondering what it is that I did wrong, how my countless hours of studying and abundant all-nighters could fail me and leave me in an academic grave with dirt already being tossed onto my GPA.

So, I do what I always do in a crisis.

I call my dad.

～

My first failure left me marked for the rest of my life, quite literally. The scar on my left cheek that makes me irreversibly asymmetrical is a constant reminder of this moment of stark, horrific, unforgettable failure. I have been told I make this story far more dramatic than it needs to be, but, again, to be fair, it left me scarred for life, quite literally.

I ran into a stop sign while learning to ride my bike. I took it as the universe telling me I didn't need this particular skill. Yes, feel free to laugh it up. You wouldn't be the first. You, however, will never live up to the first.

As I laid on my back, with the world around me spinning like the front wheel of my toppled bicycle, I gazed up at the bright blue sky through clouds that I could only imagine resulted from a stuffed animal massacre and squinted my eyes at the glaring, scolding summer sun. I could hear laughter. And I knew it wasn't my own. I knew because there was blood dripping down my cheek and onto my lips and anyone with that metallic taste in their mouth wouldn't be laughing, not at the age of six. Not lying on the sidewalk, where your blood was filling in the indent left by some kid's name and handprint.

I should've been crying, but instead, I was too preoccupied being scolded by the sun to cry. Too preoccupied with the sound of someone else's laughter to make a sound myself. Then I heard the footsteps, not rushed but light, faint, almost easy to miss. The sun stopped its screaming when her figure shielded my eyes.

"Hey there, y'alright?" she asked through bubbles of laughter, wiping tears away from her own eyes with one hand while offering the other to me, "I'm sorry for laughing, I just can't help it." Had she been sorry, she would've stopped laughing. She didn't.

I took her hand anyway and she helped me to my feet.

"Heya, you're the new neighbor girl, ain'tcha? My dad told me there was a girl my age around here. Well, I guess really, I'm the new neighbor girl, 'cause you were here first," she rocked back and forth from the balls of her feet to the very edges of her heels.

Her shoes weren't tied though I couldn't judge because mine were still Velcro. She wore mismatched socks all the way up to her scuffed knees, a pleated skirt, and a bright yellow tee. Her smile, though missing a few teeth, was brighter than the sun and whiter than the clouds. One of her pigtails was in danger of falling apart entirely.

I was too busy filling my head with what would be, moments from then, memories filed away for safekeeping to speak.

"What's your problem? Cat gotcha tongue or did ya knock it out when ya crashed?" she giggled. I was annoyed that she was laughing, I remember that because I wasn't and if I wasn't laughing that meant she couldn't be laughing with me.

She could only be laughing at me.

My red-streaked cheek grew red of its own accord, as did its partner, and I was stuck standing on that block of sidewalk as if the kid's name were freshly written. I felt trapped. My legs didn't want to move as much as I did. A bad habit of mine is that, when I feel trapped, I can't help but cry, whether I want to or not, so that's what I did. Tears evaporated off of my burning cheeks.

She laughed for a few more moments before she even noticed, but I can't really blame her. My gaze had become plastered to the ground so the only way she could even tell was by the puddles that were taking form around my feet.

"Hey, I'm sorry, I didn't mean to make ya cry…" she placed her hand on my shoulder. When I met her gaze, she gasped, turning even paler which should have been impossible. "You're bleeding, c'mon." Before I knew it, she was tugging me along and I was staggering behind her. She said we'd come back for the bike later.

I didn't know that she'd be tugging me around for over a decade. I truly had no idea what I'd gotten myself into.

"Don't worry, my parents aren't home, but I know where the band-aids are. In case of 'mergency, y'know?" she said as she dragged me inside. The door was unlocked. Only now do I question what she was doing outside in the first place.

"Uh, yeah, okay," I said with my typical talent for the art of conversation. She shoved me down on the couch and ran off to find the band-aids. I always envied how much nicer her house was than mine. Though, I couldn't help but notice that it didn't look lived in, just for display. Later she told me she envied my house because it was a home.

"I already told ya don't worry, you're gonna be just fine, okay? There's no reason to cry anymore," she said, dropping bits of wrapper behind her as she peeled the band-aid open. She pressed the adhesive against my cheek, careful to center the actual bandage on the wound. Rather attentive for such a young age.

Maybe she was used to putting on band-aids. I'd never had the nerve to ask. "There ya go, good as new!" she beamed as she gave my cheek a light tap.

It was a strange situation, being in a random girl's house receiving medical care from some kind of Doc McStuffins, so the blame cannot rest entirely on me for my lack of well-thought-out responses. Very poignantly, with a great amount of skill, I responded, "Thanks."

She laughed again, but this time I joined in a bit, softly, under my breath. "That was pretty funny, you falling like that. I don't think your bike likes ya very much," she grinned with her missing teeth.

I gave a real laugh, and only then did I feel the air rush through a spot it couldn't have before, one once blocked by a tooth. I raised my tongue to feel the exposed, bleeding gum and realized that was why my mouth still had a lingering metallic taste. In doing so, I gasped, and with wide eyes, burst out, "I lost a tooth!" I probably had a slight lisp as I spoke, but I was too astonished to take note of it.

She, rather unimpressed as she'd already lost her two front teeth, tilted her head at me and giggled, "Well where is it?"

"How would I know?" I said incredulously, only able to think about how much I wanted a glass of water, so I could wash the taste of iron off my tongue. I'd take anything to wash the sound of her laughing at me out of my ears but sadly that remains stuck with me to this day. "Near my bike, prob'ly."

"Ya coulda swallowed it," she said and nudged my side.

"What? No way," I shook my head. I didn't even want to think about that but, in reality, I probably did swallow my first lost tooth. You can't imagine the look on my face when the tooth fairy came regardless. It took me some time to figure out that mystery.

"Oh c'mon, it's the only answer. Ya swallowed your tooth when you hit that stop sign. We should really get your bike, huh? Before the carpet elves steal it?" she said as she headed to the door.

"The what?" I asked as I followed after her. This time I got to laugh at her.

"Oh, y'know, the little guys that take your toys away if you leave them on the ground and don't put them away, the carpet elves. Those guys are real mean. They'll take anything, I bet they're strong enough to take your bike, but it might take 'em a while," she said all of this with such seriousness that I had to stop laughing. She had me pretty convinced, perhaps carpet elves were real, and I just didn't know about them.

I followed her back to my bike and the scene of my first failure. She helped me wheel it back home because, even though I told her it was only a few houses down, she insisted I was injured and in need of assistance.

"What's your name, new girl?" she asked once we were finally in my driveway. Only then did I realize we didn't even know each other's name. It felt odd because even that short encounter made her feel like some sort of integral part in my life, something that'd always just kind of been there.

"Oh, uh, I'm Jane Carter," I said, and she took my hand without me even offering it.

"Well, Jane Carter," she said as she shook my hand, "You're going to be my best friend from now on, okay?" She tilted her head so the pigtail that was falling apart actually did and left tresses of hair water-falling over her pale-yellow sleeved shoulder.

"Yeah, uh, okay," I blinked, stunned by the proposition. Well, it was more a demand than a proposition, but one I was willing to accept.

She grinned, nodded once, and went on her way. She was already down the driveway and past the mailbox before I realized I still didn't know who she was.

"Hey, wait!" I called after her, standing in the driveway, clutching the handlebars of my bike, which would soon be collecting dust near my dad's toolbox in the garage, "What's your name?"

She glanced back at me with her big bright eyes and a toothless grin. "Thea Alderson."

～

That next Monday I learned Thea Alderson was good for her word. She ran up to me before class as we were all lining up out in the cold and flung her arms around me, her plush purple parka vest flattening in the embrace. I staggered back, wrapping my arms around her to regain some sense of stability, both physical and mental, as I realized she wasn't kidding.

"Hiya Jane!" she chimed, as if she hadn't seen me mere days ago and as if we hadn't just officially met mere days ago.

"Whoa, heya Thea," I laughed slightly because I have a bad habit of laughing at unexpected things. It doesn't always turn out as well as it does in this instance. The news that my great grandfather died being met with laughter made me look like a pretty shitty great-grandchild, after all.

"Heya Thea," she mimicked me, "Y'know, I like the sound of that. Maybe I could have a tv show and that could be what it's called!"

"Well, what would it be about?" I tilted my head.

"Oh, I dunno, that's for someone else to figure out silly! The star never does the work!" she laughed as she nudged my side.

I chuckled and shook my head, taking in how much of an oddball she was. Honestly, at first, I didn't think this whole best friend thing was going to last. She just seemed too fun for someone like me, like keeping me around would be a burden for her or something. We ended up balancing each other out though. We complemented each other, a two-piece puzzle.

She, for example, despised Gushers.

I know, what kind of kid could hate little gems made of chewy sugar, filled with even more liquid sugar, right? Well, like I said, she was an oddball.

She saved me a spot next to her for lunch because she decided I was her best friend. I didn't complain, I usually ate lunch quietly sitting by myself, so this was an upgrade across the board. She had one of those really cool metal lunchboxes, at least I always thought they were really cool, cooler than my brown paper bags. Only now do I truly appreciate how my parents would draw on them every morning, making a brown paper bag into a work of art just for me. I miss those stupid paper bags.

"Hey, so whatcha got?" Thea nudged my side, a growingly common occurrence it seemed.

I emptied the contents of the bag onto the table, it was an apple, a granola bar, a fruit punch juice box, and a peanut butter and banana sandwich because those were my favorite.

"Ooh, I'll trade you these for the apple!" Thea said and held out the pack of Gushers. I'd never seen them before, my parents didn't like buying things that probably didn't contain anything but chemicals, which makes no sense because everything just contains chemicals, but they intrigued me, nonetheless.

"What are those?" I asked, taking in the bright yellow packaging and the strange name.

"Oh, it's some kind of fruit snack. I don't really like them, they're really sweet," Thea said and shrugged a shoulder. Too sweet piqued my interest because what could too sweet possibly mean? She was a kid, sugar was supposed to be the number one thing on her mind, how could they be *too* sweet?

I pursed my lips, contemplating, before finally answering with a "Deal." The next few moments of my life were glorious. I can still taste those sugary gems of absolute magic if I think back to it. I swear, as a kid, I thought I had discovered actual magic the first time I bit into a Gusher and that weird ass sugar syrup gushed out. Thea laughed as I felt my soul transcend to a whole new level of being and questioned how the hell she could hate these magnificent pieces of mankind's handiwork.

"I guess you like them?" she laughed, "Well, my dad packs them for me every day. How 'bout we always trade?"

Shoveling little sugar gems into my mouth, I nodded feverously. That was a deal I could not refuse. It was one I would later regret but my dentist sure as hell would appreciate several cavities later. If I'm being perfectly honest, it was worth it because, from that day forward, Thea and I always traded: she gave me her Gushers and I gave her whatever piece of fruit I had.

It was a symbiotic relationship.

Our friendship didn't stop at the trading of snacks, however. Thea was dead set on being actual best friends and I went along with whatever she said, really. When she wanted to play on the monkey bars at recess, I was there, hanging on for dear life because I was horrible at them. When she wanted to finally get the two swings our school's playground had to offer, I was sprinting to them alongside her. When she wanted to get one of the coveted "good balls" for four square, I was rushing to the front of the line with her. And when she didn't want to play, we sat by the fence, talking about all sorts of random and wonderful things.

We talked about how we'd grow up to be secret agents, saving the world, while solving crimes like Sherlock and Watson and being princesses of our own made-up country with the rule that every citizen must wear light-up shoes on Monday to make the day less terrible. Our imagined future selves really were something else. They were anything but practical, but at least we were still so full of dreams. And no matter how crazy they sounded, we were still together.

We always talked about building our own secret hideout, though, right in Thea's backyard. After watching some cartoons and seeing a treehouse, we decided we needed to have one as well. We even drew one up, designed it together, and everything. We were picky about every single detail. Where the windows went, what the stairs up to it looked like, where everything went from the beanbag chairs to the radio, we even added a fireman's pole as the way down just because it was awesome. Just thinking of how cool it would be, having a space all our own, able to do whatever we wanted whenever we wanted, was too much for us to really fathom.

That's why, when her dad surprised her by building her that exact dream treehouse, we just about lost our minds.

Immediately after he showed her his big project, she was on my porch, slamming on the doorbell. My mom answered the door, laughing because she knew who it'd be even before opening it. I think she was glad I had a friend.

Thea said a quick hello and ran inside. I was watching tv, eating a bowl of cereal because it was a late Sunday morning and there was no better way to spend it. That's what I thought anyway until Thea dragged me all the way through her house into her backyard, just screaming with excitement and gripping me by my shoulders to shake me. "Jane look! Look at it! It's our hideout!"

I finally got a good look at it, and she was right. It looked like our drawing had come to life and put itself in her backyard. We were screaming about it for a solid five minutes before we climbed up the stairs, got to take in the inside, and screamed some more.

Her dad must have gotten ahold of our plans because even the color of the walls was exact: half a pale fuchsia, half a dark seafoam. The bean bag chairs were the red and blue ones we'd always imagined sitting in and discussing the many gruesome crimes we'd solve, ancient relics we'd rediscover, and supervillains' plots we'd foil. Of course, none of this came to pass, but we had the treehouse hideout just in case it ever did.

If I had to quantify the amount of time we spent up there, I'd say we spent years sitting in those bean bag chairs and talking about nothing and everything.

It took a while for us to ever talk of something of substance though. You wouldn't guess it but, when it comes to herself, Thea is a very private person. While she has no problem spilling your secrets to the whole world, she keeps hers under lock and key. That particular lock being welded shut while the key had been tossed in a dead fish and then fed to a shark.

She was a princess in a tower, perhaps put there by some malevolent force, or perhaps barricading herself away. It drove me absolutely insane that I couldn't figure out which it was, much less be the knight that rescued her.

⚬⚬⚬

It was late, raining like it did for the few months between fall and winter that it wasn't snowing. It was a school night and in fifth grade, my bedtime on a school night was nine-thirty, which I only occasionally tried to fight. It was twelve thirty-two when there was a knock on our front door. My mother was up working on one of her many tough sells. This one was a murder-suicide in which the father took the lives of his wife and two kids, wrote in their blood that some god of death compelled him to do so, and then killed himself.

Considering the blood was still stained on the white walls and the agency refused to paint over it because it would ruin the house's quote-unquote authenticity, no one could blame her for it being difficult. She did, however, end up getting it sold to some very macabre newlyweds. And yes, before you ask, she did not spare any details when telling me work stories. Possibly why I'm a bit of a shit show but my dad says it's only one of the reasons, which I suppose is reassuring.

Anyway, reading about a gruesome murder and possible demonic possession had my mom a bit on edge so she wasn't quick to open the door, but she was quick to snap from murder house-mode to maternal-mode the second she saw Thea standing there in her mismatched pajamas, missing one slipper, clutching a mud-stained blanket.

I'm guessing my mom said something along the lines of, "Oh dear, you're going to catch your death out there," as she ushered her inside. She came to get me because she knew Thea would likely be more comfortable with me around.

Only in high school would she be comfortable enough to sit on the couch and chat with my mom, drinking tea, before I even got home. That was a common sight during the later years of our friendship, the two of them kicking back, or Thea making fun of my brothers, or consulting my dad about one of his anonymous animal patients. Sometimes it even felt like she was more welcome in my house than I was, but I didn't mind, or at least I tried not to.

I woke up to my mother gently shaking my shoulder, telling me Thea was over and not to be too rude or questioning. She said it seemed like Thea was a bit distressed. She kept telling me how to act even though, to me, everything she said seemed like pretty obvious. I guess she just expected me to be more of a child than I was, or than I thought I was.

I rubbed the sand out of my eyes, grabbed a pair of spare pajamas that I knew would fit Thea's slender, bordering on scrawny, physique. She wasn't hard to please, in the state she was in, she just nodded once, thanked me, and headed to the bathroom to change and dry off with the towel my mom fetched for her. I asked her what was going on, but she said she didn't have a clue, just that Thea showed up on our doorstep. She didn't say much else other than that she needed to make a quick call, which I'm sure was to Thea's parents.

Taking a seat on the couch, I waited patiently for my best—and to be honest, only—friend to come back out and tell me what was going on. I thought about demanding answers because I didn't like how worried my mom seemed and I wanted to fix things. I thought about forcing her to talk to me just to get the whole mess sorted out so we could all go back to bed and back to dreaming of who knows what grandiose ideas our childish minds could conjure up.

And then she stepped back into the living room, dead silent, and I could tell by the look on her eyes, despite them being glued to the floor, that she, in no way, shape, or form, wanted to talk about whatever had caused her to end up at our front door.

Instead of prying as I had planned, I patted the cushion beside me and remained quiet. She took my offer of the seat laying her head against my shoulder.

No sound bounced off the walls we stared blankly at. The room was a void of silence, and we were void of voices until my mother returned, finishing up her call with a "Goodnight, Mr. Alderson. It's no trouble at all." As she stuffed her phone into her pocket, she turned to us, running a hand through her hair and pushing up her glasses before speaking. "Thea, you're going to be our guest for the night. Just because this is a sleepover doesn't mean it's not a school night though," she teased.

Thea's eyes lit up and mine did as well. Our first sleepover, on a school night, how crazy was my mom to let that happen? Well, I guess not that crazy because we ended up going to bed shortly after.

It was 1:07 am, or so my light-up Hello Kitty clock said, and I couldn't believe we were up so late. Thea and I shared my bed, each facing the opposite direction. We hadn't spoken much besides small jokes about how everyone should be jealous we got to have a sleepover on a school night and none of them were invited, how we were the coolest. It was 1:08 am when Thea broke our near-total silence.

"Hey Jane…?" she whispered.

"Can you see the stars through that window?

"Yeah, Thea?"

"I'm going to be one someday."

"Sure you are," I replied, looking back to see if she'd turned to face me. She hadn't. Another brief stint of silence followed, broken only by the rustling of the blanket and Thea once more.

"Thanks for…having me over…" she said, a small sniffle breaking her sentence into two parts.

"Uh, yeah, of course," I said, "Get some sleep, we still have school in the morning, and we've got a lot of gloating to do, y'know?"

She laughed slightly, "Yeah, okay, goodnight, Jane…"

"G'night T," I said back. It was 1:09 am when I finally shut my eyes and let them stay shut.

I used to wonder if that night was just another one of my many failures. A better friend would have asked, right? Then again, maybe that's what being a friend is all about. Just being there. Going through it together.

CHAPTER 5

Concession Stance

With my first of many college likely failures past me, I decided to avoid sinking into post-midterms depression as best I could. I thought back to the things I enjoyed before I became this soulless paper-producing scantron-coloring robot. It took some time to revert back to a semi-normal person, with interests and hobbies because let's face it, I wasn't normal to begin with, but I managed.

I remembered that I enjoyed movies, but not having someone to go with made the theatre a no-go and Netflix had consumed enough of my time as is. I thought about going for a run but remembering the spontaneous rainy-day table hurdling with Eddie quickly snapped me back to my unathletic reality. And then I blanked.

Schoolwork had consumed so much of my time for the first few weeks of college that I completely forgot what hobbies were. And then I realized I never really had hobbies to begin with. Theatre took up most of my time.

But luckily, there was a production nearby and, theatre having been my only hobby for so long, it wasn't hard to convince myself that I may enjoy watching a show as much as putting one on. Strutting to my last-minute seat from which the stage was nearly imperceptible, not that I desperately needed to see the shabby community theatre set pieces or overdressed actors, I took a glance at the playbill. As it was *Le Malentendu* by Albert Camus, I clung loosely to the hope that my four years of high school French would be enough to help me skate by, but I only got as far as the title and, by the time the curtain closed, the title was all that was on my mind. Well, that and the peanut M&M's I'd bought before the show but forgotten about. When I opened the bag and poured a couple into my palm, the colors melted off and stained my skin in a way that was all too familiar, reminding me of my first near-crush.

~

He may not have been the one to seal the deal on my return to that chaotic place, but Edison Bishop certainly was a factor in the decision, both positive and negative.

There was something about him, some sort of magnetic passion, that made you want to follow him. Some would call Eddie a natural-born leader. I would call him a natural-born casualty, diving headfirst into anything and everything he thought was worthwhile and more often than not ending up hurt by the outcome. Regardless, I could not avoid this polarity.

But I wanted nothing less than to kiss him.

It's not like he wasn't attractive because, objectively, he was. His symmetrical face with bright eyes, fair skin, his lava-like curls, and his athletic body would drive anyone crazy. At first glance that is. But the only thing to drive me crazy after an initial glance was him. He was always off the walls, bouncing between conversation and conversation. He had a talent for making whoever he was talking to feel listened to without letting them get a single word in. And looking back on it, I supposed I had a talent for never getting a single word in.

And, that afternoon, after I left my dreaded AP World History class behind me and stopped by the vending machine to pick up a much-needed pick-me-up—peanut M&M's, my regular—and sauntered into the theatre, that's just what he did.

"Ah, so my Juliet has returned once again!" Eddie cheered as he swung an arm around my shoulders and swiped a few M&M's from the pack, paying little to no mind to my displeasure. "I worry day and night that you'll change your mind and stop showing up, you know?"

"Oh, I'm sure you do," I rolled my eyes and shrugged his arm off my shoulders, taking a seat in the stands and waiting for Mitchell. Thea to come out and tell us which scenes we were blocking and reading for the week. I had my fingers continually crossed that none of the kissing scenes were on the agenda.

Eddie, clearly not taking my cues, plopped down in the seat beside me but threw his knees over the edge so his whole body would be facing me. "I really do. It keeps me up at night. Do you see these bags under my eyes?" He pointed at them for good measure, "You know what caused them? Sleep-deprivation. You know who caused them? You. So, if you even had a shred of compassion for me, you'd say it already, that you aren't going to just up and leave us with half a leading cast." He crossed his arms and pouted, melodramatic as ever.

"I haven't left yet, have I?" I countered, "Besides, I'd spend more of those sleepless hours worrying about your lines than about me, Mr. 'thou canst not teach me to…line?' I like to think anyone be taught, if they're willing to study, that is." As lame as it was, I smirked at my own "clever" remark.

He was not half as amused as I was, however. "Not everyone has mastery of memory like you, okay?" he huffed as he tugged on one of his particularly tightly-wound curls, "How did you get the whole thing committed, anyway?"

I'd been memorizing lines as long as Thea's been writing them, but nobody else needed to know of our symbiosis, so I gave him a half-hearted shrug and turned my attention to the stage, where Mitchell stood, clearing his throat to hush the crowd, with Thea by his side. I poured a few more M&M's into my hand and listened as I ate them in the primary order of color and the subset order of size. Thea had always made fun of me for eating M&M's like that. If she knew I peeled the chocolate off in my mouth, ate that, and then ate the peanut, I think she'd choke on her own onslaught of teasing remarks.

"Alright everyone, I'm sure you're wondering why we've gathered you all here. There's no easy way to say this but you're fired," Mitchell said and, with a soft and disappointed sigh, responded to the unamused silence of the room, "Oh, my bad, wrong notes. Crew, you're on backdrops today. Listen to every word that comes out of Valerie's mouth like it were gospel, she's never been wrong so don't try to argue."

That, unlike his initial joke, got a small snicker from the crew, as Valerie, while gifted with a master's eye for aesthetics, was not without fault. The prior week, she'd spent three hours debating if the sleeves of Benvolio's tunic should have been pacific mist or ivory cream. A perfectionist to the very core, she let hours slip through her fingers like sand, which was in fact the only color she determined his sleeves should not be. That was for Romeo's pants exclusively.

"Tech," Mitchell moved on, "Focus on lights for Act I and sounds for the Benvolio and Tybalt clash need to be run through for an initial timing check at least once. The clanking of swords can sound far too similar to the bin of forks we recorded if not timed out just right." With that, Victor and the other tech members sunk away to their dark and, in my opinion, dingey abode to get down to business.

The atmosphere certainly suited him, but other than that, I couldn't gather why Victor wasn't a part of the crew with Valerie. My theory was that the two of them would end up covered in paint if left together, playful paintbrush strokes having turned into an all-out war. A similar theory applies to if they were both in tech, but that dark room would lend itself to even less savory behavior.

"And cast," Mitchell said with a final clasp of his hand and a show of bravado, "Benvolio and Tybalt, I want you working on your swordsmanship but for everyone else, I think it's about time we start testing the waters with Act 1 Scene 5." My stomach dropped to my feet. Anything but that scene, I'd mentally begged and pleaded but alas no gods heard my prayers and deemed me fit for mercy.

Eddie kicked my heel to get my attention and I turned to see his lips playful pursed like a fish. I'm sure I paled a few shades past dead and the instant Mitchell dismissed us to get to work, I speed-walked off to get that damn corset on, which Thea insisted I wear while rehearsing. It was, for the first time, not the thing I dreaded the most that day.

Thea must not have seen me run off because she didn't come in to assist me in getting the torture device on as she normally did but, somehow, I managed. It definitely didn't help slow the quick and nervous breaths rattling in the cage of my ribs. My heart was beating against the bars, a deranged prisoner. I couldn't help but be scared out of my wits, it was the day I'd, whether I liked it or not, have my first kiss.

It's not like I'd never had the opportunity before. I had those same camp stories everyone had, those swift summer crushes, but I, unlike most, never acted on any of them. And now, looking back on it, I'm glad I hadn't. Having to tell the story of my first kiss as a brace-faced camp kid with another brace-faced camp kid whose name was, get this, Herbert is a hell I, fortunately, avoided damning myself to. Especially given the legends that we would've gotten our metal mouths stuck together.

But, in that moment, it was the fear of the unknown that petrified me. It was the idea that, in an instant, I'd go from not knowing to knowing even if it wasn't a big deal, even if it didn't mean anything and was just meant to be our characters, not us, sharing a tender moment, that shook me to my very core. It was change.

That and just why did it have to be Eddie?

He was everything I wasn't, and it drove me insane. He was like a fly bussing right by my ear that I just couldn't kill, a constant annoyance just buzz-buzz-buzzing away my grip on sanity. He had this ability to walk into a room and turn everyone's attention to him, taking the stage in any conversation on any topic and commanding it like a tyrant. He made himself known with his grandiose sense of self and loud vocal announcement of his presence, whether he meant to or not, that drew all eyes to him. He was a statue in any crowd, easy to pick out and gilded in enough gold to blind everyone around him.

I was the shadow cast by that statue and preferred to be so. Attention was not something I craved, unlike him. I didn't need everyone to know I was in a room when I walked in, in fact, I was happier when they didn't. It was easier to get people to show you their genuine selves when they forgot you were even there.

Eddie didn't seem to care about seeing or even being genuine, always a caricature.

At least I, even when pulled to a perfect figure with that damn corset, remained genuinely Jane, discomfort, annoyance, and all.

I opened the door right as he reached to knock, and we were left face to face.

"Hey, you were taking a while, everything good?" Eddie asked.

"Yep, everything's great, perfect actually, I'm going to go check on our cousins though, make sure they're not at each other's throats, okay bye," I said so fast it seemed like the words were just one continuous stream.

"But…but they're supposed to be at each other's throats?" he asked, confused, and, to my dismay, followed after me, "We've got a scene to rehearse too, you know!"

"Oh, we can do that any time. Besides, I doubt you even have your lines down quite yet. Why don't you go run those?" I responded, headed closer to the sound of clashing swords as our rationales clashed.

"Well then why don't you come run them with me?" he suggested.

I assured him I would, later, but he persisted until we were watching the clashing swords of our casted cousins. If there's anything I've learned from that day, the constant whacking of wooden practice swords does nothing to calm one's nerves and instead elevate them to battlefield survival instincts. Everyone becomes an enemy.

His hand on my shoulder became a gun pressed to my back and I, choosing fight over flight, armed myself with a wooden practice sword and swung myself out of his reach. In a moment of pure absurdity, I said the only thing I could think to say that would make me seem both less and more insane. "En garde!"

"Looks like the lady wants in on the fight!" Benvolio chimed, taking my actions as an opportunity for improv.

"I'll protect my dear cousin with both blood and steel!" Tybalt said and charged to my side as Benvolio charged to smite me.

Eddie, always happy to oppose the status quo and go far off script, drew a blade himself and positioned himself so he was back-to-back with me. "Cousin, you will not slay my Juliet!"

"She is not yours, for you are a Montague," Tybalt shifted his attention to Eddie and their swords clashed, foreshadowing the need for hours of practice for scenes yet rehearsed. Eddie was no swordsman and crafting him into one would be teaching a fish to walk. I, clashing swords with Benvolio, learned of my affinity for the blade, oddly enough. However, our clash did not last long as Benvolio saw Eddie getting slaughtered and ran to his aid, taking Tybalt's attention for himself. Which left me, armed, face to face with my supposed Romeo.

He, lost in the absurdity of the moment, did not waste a moment on hesitation when our swords clashed under my prompting. So, there we were, Romeo and Juliet, two star-crossed lovers, attempting to end the other's life. What a twist of fate. Even in that moment, the irony was not lost on me.

It took Mitchell's loud and heart-stopping clap to drag us all off the battleground and back to the stage. "What are my leads doing clashing blades?" he asked, bewildered. My sword dropped to the ground with an anti-climactic thud.

"She started it," Eddie said, the reality of how stupid we were acting crashing on him like a curtain to the stage post-show. He flushed, embarrassed to be seen in such a foolish light by his idol, embarrassed to have put himself in that light in the first place.

"And you played along," Mitchell said, "While your swordsman-ship was full of energy, I've been waiting for you both to come show me that energy on the stage. Now, if you're done playing around, I'd appreciate it if you'd start to take things a little more seriously. Take five to cool down and, when you finally start acting your ages, get to work." He huffed and went off to his office, likely to question his choice in casting me.

Eddie, the most heartbroken I'd even seen him, cleaned up the carnage of our battle and left me to watch as Tybalt and Benvolio took their places and went back to rehearsing their actual, intentional fight scene. I stood, shell-shocked, for a few moments before heading out for fresh air and, as per usual, it was raining. It was never not raining it seemed, but at least the rain was a nice little scenic reflection of my mental state.

I sank down against the brick wall, happy for the slight overhang of the theatre's roof that kept my torso dry yet allowed my outstretched legs to get polka-dotted in raindrops. I closed my eyes, sitting in si-lence for a few moments before I heard the door open and saw him, in the corner of my eye, sink down beside me. I didn't pay him any mind until I realized he was holding something out to me: a new pack of peanut M&M's.

"Sorry about earlier, I guess I forgot to ask before taking some. I do that sometimes," he rubbed the back of his neck.

I hesitated before taking the pack and tore it open, pouring a few in his outstretched hand before he retracted it. "It's alright," was all I said before pouring a few in my palm and putting one in my mouth, peeling the chocolate off with my teeth before eating the peanut in my special neurotic way. I was about three M&M's in before I noticed that Eddie was watching me.

"What?" I asked with a mouthful of chocolate.

"Do you peel the chocolate off and eat the peanut too?" he asked.

"Well yeah of cour—wait… too? You do that?" I wasn't sure if he was playing a trick on me and teasing my neuroticism, so I refused to seem overly stunned.

"Yeah, I've never met someone else who eats them like that," Eddie said, smiling in a way that made him seem—for the first time I'd seen—genuine. I must have been staring at him, dumbfounded, because he laughed a bit and turned away, not before I caught a look at the chocolate all stuck in his teeth. I couldn't help but laugh a bit as well.

By the time he spoke again, my palms had already begun to dye the color of the M&M's as the candy shells began to melt with the mixed conditions of the moisture in the air and my body heat. That imagine, my hands clutching rainbows, was one a made a mental note to doodle next time I was bored in AP World History, which was sure to be sooner rather than later. Before I could get too deep into the planning phase of my next mid-class trip to the clouds, Eddie's voice pulled me back down.

"Well, um, I'm sure Mitchell is waiting for us," he said as he stood up and wiped the dirt off his pants, "I'm gonna head in and start running over some of my lines. Feel free to join me once you're ready." I saw him run a hand through his curls before the door closed behind him.

My mind started racing the second he was gone. Sure, he was a nice guy, but I simply wasn't interested. Yes, there was the whole moment with the M&M's, and we even ate them the same way and learned a bit about each other, but that didn't change the fact that he unendingly annoyed me.

While he was growing on me—like a rash might I add—he had yet to be a friend and I certainly did not want him to be anything more. I couldn't have him getting the wrong idea. By this point, I'd accepted that I'd have to kiss him but I sure as hell wasn't going to let it be me kissing him. It was Juliet kissing Romeo, nothing more. Jane and Eddie were simply part of the equation, they were certainly not to be the output.

And then my stomach clenched at the most horrendous thought. The candy, the constant touchy-feely-ness of Eddie, it all came crashing down on me at once. Oh god, I thought, what if he thinks it's more than a role?

And then, for just a moment, I thought of something even worse. What if I did?

Don't worry, that thought didn't last long. I knew I'd have to let him down easy, even if I wanted to let him down hard. Breaking his heart is the last thing I wanted to do and besides it would make every rehearsal even more awkward if there were any hard feelings. Thea was doing her best to make everything run smoothly and I, as her best friend, would be damned if it was my fault things went to shit.

I knew what I had to do, I had to get in there, smile, run the lines, and, before the kiss, let him know that there was nothing going on between us. It was harsh, sure, but it had to be done. After a moment of steeling my nerves, tightening my corset to keep the butterflying in my stomach from fluttering up and out of my throat, I went in with only one mission in mind: to clear up that whole misunderstanding.

Mitchell was waiting on me, tapping his watch with just enough annoyance that he was sure I'd notice. I did. I hurried to my place and the scene began. By the time the dreaded moment arrived, we'd already run through our lines again and again.

"Carter, where is your energy? You're all over the place. Give me Juliet, not whoever this is supposed to be," he'd say every time before making us start over. His patience was wearing thin, and I knew I had to calm down and just say my lines, clear Jane out of my head, let Juliet in.

"C'mon Jane, I've seen you do better," I could hear her say, and we were back in the treehouse, and she was throwing lines my way. Sometimes I was a pirate, a mailman, even a dog, but I could play any character and she always had a way of knowing when my head wasn't in the right place, that creative space where Jane disappears and whoever it is that I need to be comes forward.

This time, though, she didn't have to say it. She had just walked back in the room after making sure tech and crew and the rest of the cast were doing whatever needed to be done and all she had to do was give me a look. *C'mon Jane, I know you can do better*, her eyes said.

The first script she'd ever written was a one-man play because even at eleven years old she was smart enough to know she didn't have any other cast members and there was only so much I was willing to do for her. *The Last Girl on Earth*, she'd called it. It was going to be a hit, just watch, she told me. God, we were up in that treehouse rehearsing for hours every day, putting on a play for an audience of leaves and branches, the occasional squirrel popping in during intermission.

It was a never-ending script really, because every time we reached the last line, she'd always add something. Some sort of twist that would keep the show going. Once, it was that one of those squirrels held a time travel device and if I could get my hands on it, I could go back to before I was the only girl left. She was still apologizing for the scratches and the bites, and the rabies shot that quickly followed that bit of improv and I held it over her head whenever I wanted a sip of her iced coffee or a couple of her fries.

"Hey T," I turned to her one day, years later, as she jotted down a few more lines to a new, much more refined and, to be frank, much more compelling script. My eyes had caught sight of the notebook she'd kept *The Last Girl on Earth* in, so over-used that we had to staple the pages back into it to keep them from flying off when a strong enough breeze came through the windows.

"Yeah?" she chewed on the end of her pen, her eyes still on the pages in front of her.

"Why'd you never end it?"

"Hmm?" Thea looked up, tilting her head.

"*The Last Girl on Earth*. Why'd you never end it?" I asked again.

She laughed slightly, her cheeks flushing. "Oh gosh, what made you think of that old thing?" She twirled a strand of hair around the pen.

"Stop avoiding the question," I said, shifting so my chin was resting on my knee. "Why'd you never let it end?"

"Promise you won't laugh?"

"Sure."

"No really, you need to promise."

"Okay, okay, I promise."

She took a deep breath, "Well, I was worried if I ended it, *this* would end with it."

"*This*?" I blinked, not quite understanding her.

"Y'know, *this*. The treehouse, the scripts, my one-man cast, and crew. Everything we've got up here all came to be because of that thing, and I thought if I ended it, *this*, well, *you'd* end too. Stop coming around as often and all," she sighed.

I broke my promise and started to chuckle.

"Hey! I told you no laughing!" She was beet red like she'd get when she'd been out in the sun for too long with her printer paper complexion.

I wiped my tears away, apologizing, "T, c'mon, you know that never would have happened, right? I didn't care about the stupid thing, I came here all the time because of *you*!"

She hesitated for a moment before her laughter accompanied mine. That was the day we thought up an ending for the damn thing. *The Last Girl on Earth* needed a new title by that final scene when she found another girl, blonde with printer paper complexion, and they became the last *girls* on Earth.

I took a breath and when Mitchell said action, I went right up to that space where Jane vanished to whenever I was being someone else. I didn't need to look to know Thea was smiling. Mitchell didn't stop us before the kiss arrived and I, just in time, pulled myself back into my body to say, "Wait, Eddie, there's something I need to tell you…"

"I'm gay," he blurted out.

"I don't like you like that, wait… What did you just say?" I stole Thea's complexion.

"Oh no, this is exactly what I was afraid of!" Eddie burst out laughing, "You really didn't know? I knew there had to be a reason you'd been acting so strange. Look, Jane, you're great and all, but you're just not my type."

"You're not mine either! That's what I was trying to tell you!" I hid my face in shame.

Mitchell, meanwhile, was no help when it came to my embarrassment as he was laughing his ass off. Even Thea was in tears.

"You really thought Eddie liked you? Why didn't you just come to me? I could've cleared things up straight away," she said through wheezes and gasps for air.

"Okay, look, glad that's cleared up. Let's just get back to the scene. Aren't you always complaining how we're on a tight schedule?" I turned to Mitchell, who, after taking a moment to compose himself, agreed. The scene went on without a hitch.

The kiss was nothing compared to the embarrassment I'd never get to escape. From that day on, whenever Eddie and I shared a pack of peanut M&M's, he was sure to remind me not to get the wrong idea.

CHAPTER 6

Closet Thoughts

My father's advice to get over those more recent failures, all of epic proportion mind you, was to grab a friend, throw on some cheap sneakers, and hit Frat Row for some drunken adventures. Not exactly the advice you'd expect from a parent to his underaged daughter, but heartfelt and comforting, nonetheless. So, I followed it, calling up the most talkative seat partner I had, who I knew would accompany me because she had yet to show up to class without a hangover, and throwing on my dingiest pair of sneakers.

The reason he suggested cheap shoes was three-fold: to avoid drink spillage, the vomit of others, and my own vomit if necessary. Good advice, but fairly misguided, as I was already well-equipped with these "nuggets of knowledge," the term he coined them as, during our phone call. I forget, sometimes, that my parents didn't have hidden cameras following me around every corner, even if they wished they did. Thanks to my years of sneaking about and being the most trustworthy of all his children, mostly because I was the only viable option for such a title with Desmond being a bit of a wild child and Norman having the makings of an evil genius if he ever decides to pursue that path, my father seemed to be under the misconception that all I did in high school was theatre.

Well, I suppose it would be more accurate to say that he believed all I did in high school was theatre. I couldn't help but reminisce about how wrong he was, and how much I missed those days, the days when the parties were full of familiar faces.

〜

We were only just starting full dress rehearsals for all cast members, but we were already committed to the after-party lifestyle. At least once a month, one of us theatre nerds would somehow manage to throw an all-out rager for cast and crew only. There was only one undisputed exception to the cast and crew-only rule but, in all fairness, he did more work for the club than all of us put together.

"Two Volatile fraps, one Karen, and three Stacey McHotness' for one quirky yet attractive actress, anyone see a quirky yet attractive actress anywhere around here?" He called out at the top of his lungs, regardless of the fact that I was sitting right in front of him on the shop's old but perfectly worn in purple crushed velvet couch.

"Oh my god, can you shut up for once," I groaned, rolling my eyes, and shaking my head at his sheer stupidity. "You can forget about the tip now," I muttered as I reached out to grab the two drink trays needed to carry all that caffeine.

"Since when do you ever tip me?" Beckett arched a brow, pulling the trays back just out of my reach.

"You're right, I'll start now," I snatched the coffee shop visor off his head and placed it backwards on my own, "Get a haircut. You look like a goddamn mop." And with that, I grabbed the drink trays and took my leave, pleased with myself for getting the final word.

"Hey, Carter, c'mon I need that back!" Beckett called out, "I'm gonna get written up for uniform violation! Again!"

"If you really want it back, come get it from Eddie's tonight," I called back and raised the lighter of the two trays in acknowledgment. As the door swung shut, I could hear him shouting about how I was going to get him fired someday. I paid him no mind though because I knew if he was going to be fired it would be because of his own incompetence. For a guy with mop-like hair, he couldn't clean for shit. He made damn good coffee though, so I secretly hoped he didn't plan on screwing up and getting fired anytime soon.

Setting one of the trays on the roof of my worn-down car, I dug around for my keys for a few moments too long for my liking and definitely had a preemptive panic attack over just the thought of losing them before my fingers finally wrapped around the cold metal keyring and accidentally nudged my alarm button. I nearly dropped a whole tray before I managed to shut off the alarm, pile into my car with my overwhelming coffee haul, and drive back to campus. My parking space of choice in the back had yet to be taken, so I breathed a sigh of relief.

With my keys between my lips and a drink tray in each hand, I meandered into the theatre to see Eddie laying on the stage, Victor having pulled over a chair to sit on, Valerie having taken her place on her throne i.e., his lap, and Thea dramatically half hanging off the edge of the stage. Their heads all whipped around to the door and Thea almost flew to me.

"Ah finally, you're back!" She said and snatched the trays from me.

"Oh yeah, I definitely feel the love. It was totally seeing me you were looking forward to, huh?" I chuckled as I put my keys back into my bag and hopped up onto the stage to take a seat. Eddie, by the time

I had gotten up there, had already finished one of the two drinks he decided to order. His perfectly balanced order was always one Karen, for energy, and one Stacey McHotness, to drown out the god-awful taste of the Karen.

"We love you, Jane, don't get it twisted. We just love coffee way more," he grinned with a whipped cream mustache as he nudged my thigh. I laugh quietly and took a sip of my Stacey McHotness as Thea gave the drink's namesakes their Volatile fraps and took her own Stacey McHotness before joining me on the stage and laying her head on my shoulder.

"Everything good, T?" I asked and ruffled her hair.

"She missed you," Valerie chimed, "Jaea for life, Thane for days." We all had a good laugh at that one. She never missed a beat when it came to pointing out how great a couple she believed we would be.

"I'm just tired, was up all-night writing, coffee is a great pick me up though," Thea said.

"Hey now, you're not allowed to be tired, party at my place, remember? This isn't some shitty, run-of-the-mill high school sleepover, alright!" Eddie pouted, "You better be wide awake when it comes around. A sleepy drunk is no fun after all." He was right, Thea couldn't be a fun drunk when she was tired, it just wasn't something she could do. "Speaking of the party, Jane," he turned to us, "Did you invite Beckett?"

"As you requested and for no other reason, yes, I did," I said firmly.

"Uh-huh, sure," Eddie grinned. I rolled my eyes and ignored him and his constant attempts to find me a match even though I didn't need or frankly want him to do so. "Alright everyone, listen up," He stood up, "Time to get serious." He took one more sip of his Stacey

McHotness before setting it down and clasping his hands together. "Time to talk booze. Personally, I don't know about you guys, but I'm in the mood to get wasted this weekend." We all whooped and hollered in agreement.

Okay, look, I'm just going to state the obvious. We were all underaged. We're all still underaged. We shouldn't have done this. It was and still is illegal. Blah, blah, blah legality and all that jazz. But also, screw that. We were young and dumb and there was no way in hell we weren't going to drink. It's just facts people.

The more you're told not to do something, the more you want to, and man were we told not to. With all the assemblies about the dangers of underage drinking, the consistent push of the fear of alcohol poisoning, and the posters telling us that an occasional drink leads to coke which leads to meth which leads to death and all that slippery slope bullshit, how were we supposed to take drinking seriously? I know they really tried to prevent us from underage drinking for our own good, but we couldn't help from taking all the corny lies and flawed logic as anything but a long string of jokes.

Regardless of how not-so-seriously we took the idea of underage drinking, we were safe. We didn't drive, we didn't get dangerously intoxicated, we took care of each other, and we made sure there was at least always one sober-ish friend, which was usually me. Don't get me wrong, I like drinking more than most, I just never minded being the responsible one and I didn't really need to drink to feel drunk around them. Their presence was a drug in its own right, just as intoxicating.

It wasn't hard to convince my parents to let me out that night, all I had to say was I was getting coffee and then going to Thea's which was true. I didn't need to lie to my parents, it was easy enough to just leave out some of the details. I *was* getting coffee and going to Thea's, after all, that just wasn't the final destination of the night. I showed up at her doorstep with two large Karen's, because we positively needed the energy that night, as well as my overnight bag to keep up the ruse of the night being nothing more than a sleepover.

She opened the door, not even bothering to set down the makeup brush and halt her work. "Ah, just what I needed! You always know!" She grinned as she took the coffee in her free hand and then stopped, seemingly shell-shocked. "Don't tell me that's what you're wearing."

"What? Is there a problem with it?" I arched a brow and tossed my bag on her couch before plopping down beside it. "Can never go wrong with a tee and jeans."

"Oh, you most certainly can!" Thea grabbed hold of my arms and, in her very familiar way, dragged me up the stairs and to her room. She shoved me into her closet and closed the door, yelling, "Don't come out of there until you've changed into something at least moderately cute, you hear that!"

"T, you're being ridiculous, you know we're not the same size in anything," I groaned, dejectedly taking a seat on the hardwood floor.

There was a silent hesitation in the air before she opened the door just a crack, peering through it, "Okay, you're not wrong, but I can't let you go just like that." She slipped inside and looked around, sifting through hanger upon hanger looking for something to 'spice up my look' as she called it.

Finally, she sighed heavily and pulled a red flannel down. "It's not much, but it'll do. Can't have you straying too far from your comfort zone but definitely cannot have you staying in it, not tonight. I know you, J, baby steps. Now, take off that ratty old thing, would you?" She pointed to my shirt.

"Excuse me?" I stammered.

"Oh, c'mon, we both know you've got a tank on underneath. You always do." She was right, so I saw no point in arguing. Begrudgingly, I stripped off the tee and tossed on the flannel. Thea rolled the sleeves up for me and grinned, "There we go, goodbye lumberjack, hello lumber-Jane." I swear I threw up a little when those words left her lips, but she laughed in her wholehearted way, eventually needing to wipe the tears from her eyes before they ruined her makeup. "Okay, now that your outfit is slightly less deplorable, let's get you dolled up," she said.

"I don't see the point in all that, we're just hanging out with friends. Watch, by the time we get there, they're all going to be too drunk to even see my face anyway," I argued, stuffing my hands in the back pockets of my jeans because I have yet to find a pair of women's jeans with front pockets deep enough to do that and not look ridiculous.

"Doesn't matter," she said and that was the only reasoning I got before I was propped up on her bathroom counter and she was smearing gunk all over my face and nearly stabbing me in the eyes with eyeliner pencils or mascara wands. "You should be used to this by now, you're going to have to wear stage makeup and it's a lot worse than this!" She scolded me for flinching so much, but I couldn't help it. Eventually, once the worst of it was over, she took out a tube of dark red lipstick and handed it to me. "You can handle this part, I have to finish getting myself all dolled up," she nudged my shoulder as she passed by me, leaving me looking in the mirror at a person I barely recognized.

It's strange, how when you don't recognize who you are, you melt away and whatever character, whatever persona, whatever personality that's been dying to slip through the cracks, gets their chance to come out and takes it. Lost in thought as I painted my lips a darker hue, I felt a hand grip my shoulder. Jolting, my hand slipped and left a rich ruby streak across my cheek and my reflection was once again my own.

"Ah, sorry, I didn't mean to mess you up!" Thea said, trying her best to retain her sincerity but unable to keep little bubbles of laughter from slipping out. As soon as I began to laugh, she did too. "You just looked so spaced out, I was trying to pull you down from the clouds," she chuckled as she fixed the mistake, "You did a pretty good job of coloring inside the lines, other than that though, so I'm beyond proud." She wore the grin of a mother watching her child take their first steps, say their first words, or tie their own shoes.

"Oh, knock it off, don't patronize me," I rolled my eyes, doing what I could to keep from smiling.

"I'm not! Trust me, you'll know when I'm poking fun at you," Thea said, bagging up her instruments of torture, then turned to me with a small smirk, "Alright, you look great, I look even better, let's get going."

"Wow, you really weren't kidding when you said I'd know," I sighed and shook my head, already going downstairs. I snatched my keys off the couch, making sure I had my wallet on me. Thea tried convincing me to carry a purse, but I think they're ridiculous. There's no point in lugging around a bag of useless shit if all you need can, be carried on you.

As she buckled up, I chugged down the rest of my coffee and wasted no time in hitting the road. We were already late as is, thanks to her. Typical T.

~

When I clutched the shiny brass door knocker, I remembered once again that Eddie was the obvious choice for party host not only for his party personality but for the prime location which he had at his disposal. His parents were gone a lot of the time, off on research trips. His father was a packaging designer, meaning his job was to make candy bars or cereal boxes jump off the shelves and into the carts of customers based on appearance alone. This, apparently, is a very well-paying job if you have the capacity to do it.

His mother was an environmental scientist, looking into biodegradable packaging, so I always thought it was nice how, be it through their careers or through their marriage, they depended on each other in a way, sustained each other. The two always traveled together, making trips around the world to, in his case, design eye-catching candy wrappers and, in hers, subsequently, clean up the waste these wrappers left behind. Like in some sort of sitcom, the husband only made a mess and the wife's sole purpose was to clean up after him. Funny how things work out.

While I was lost in the reflection of the door knocker, it was pulled just out of my reach as Eddie made his appearance. "Darlings!" he chimed in his worst snobbish voice and flung his arms around us. With his cheek brushing mine, I was close enough to smell the alcohol on his breath. He wasn't exactly the patient type, so it was just like him to get a head start. "So glad you could make it, welcome to my humble abode!" He released us to stumble inside, not-so-casually flinging the edge of his scarf back over his shoulder as he beckoned us to follow.

"Eddie, you're already yelling!" Thea half-yelled and half-laughed, "How many drinks have you had? You promised you wouldn't start without me!"

"Oh please, we both know you'll catch up in no time," Eddie leaned against her, his arm atop her head, "Everyone knows you're not the most absorbent sponge in the sink."

"What is that even supposed to mean?" she laughed at his mediocre idiom.

"Oh, c'mon T, everyone knows you're a lightweight," I said, taking in the sights and sounds of an Edison Bishop trademark party for what seemed like the millionth time, even if I'd only been to a handful of them. The music wasn't your typical high school party music, Eddie was too classy for that. Instead, his parent's record player bellowed the finest oldie records, filling the air with trumpet blares and tambourine, notes ripping the air and forcing open a portal to another decade. It always made me feel weightless, perhaps half-empty, perhaps half-full, drifting.

There were interruptions to this flight, though. The crunching of red solo cups kept me grounded. The tugging of laughter summoned me to converse, a pastime of which, in any other circumstance, I was less than fond of. Small talk was a little dog yipping at your heels to me, yet in these moments it was muzzled and much more tolerable. Perhaps it was the alcohol nipping at my ear, whispering, coercing, that bade me make myself more tolerable.

Victor and Valerie were nowhere to be seen, perhaps enjoying the other's company in some coat closet or, god forbid, a spare bedroom. I often played the role of clean-up crew at these events and there was not a chance in hell I'd clean that up. Eddie tugged Thea off to go chat with the numerous people I did not know, nor did I care to know. I preferred a tight knit circle, so it was fine, the two of them leaving me to wade through the sea of faces. I managed to spot a familiar one, something to latch onto, but of course, it had to be him.

"One of us is going to have to change."

And of course, he, too, was wearing a red flannel, unbuttoned, with the sleeves rolled up.

Beckett smiled ear to ear as he sauntered his way over to me, parting the red Solo cup sea. It was the first time I noticed the gap between his teeth and the single dimple embedded in his left cheek, though both were constellation-covered. Had I just not bothered to care before, just been too fixated on the coffee cups to notice the minute details in the face of the person handing them to me?

"Yeah, and it'd be you. You wouldn't even be here if not for me, remember?" I nudged his shoulder a bit.

"Buuut, everyone already saw me in this outfit, and it seems to me like you're, well, a little late to the party," he countered, chuckling as he nudged my shoulder back.

"Ah, c'mon, you know it's not my fault I'm late." It's true, if it'd been up to me, I would have been there helping to set up.

"I wonder who in the world it could've possibly been with absolutely no sense of time whatsoever," Beckett said and rubbed his chin, pondering. He'd known Thea and me long enough to know she ran about half an hour late, at the very least. We both laughed.

"Alright, Carter, what's the game plan here? How do we explain the outfits? Are we the secret lovers who just can't keep their mutual devotion hidden from the public eye any longer or are we the will-they-won't-they couple yet to be?"

"Obviously the latter, now, onto the important matters. Would you mind helping me find the drinks, lover boy?" I rolled my eyes at him, but the corners of my lips still found themselves curling.

"Hold on, speaking of drinks, I recall a rather snarky customer snatching my visor while picking up their order. Happen to know where that customer might be and where my visor could have ended up? I'll let you know, I barely managed to talk my way into getting off with a warning," he said, trying to feign annoyance but I could tell he wasn't.

I inhaled through my clenched teeth. "Damn, I knew I'd forgotten something. A shit to give," I chimed as I shrugged and went off to the kitchen to find something that would make the night a little more tolerable.

"Whoa, hey, seriously I do need that back," he chuckled and jogged after me. He wasn't as good at weaving through crowds as I was, as avoiding people had been one of my most coveted skills and he was lanky in a newborn giraffe kind of way, so by the time he caught up to me, I was already in the kitchen, pouring myself a glass of whatever the hell was in the punch bowl. I slid a red solo cup across the counter to him.

"Bottoms up," I smirked and chugged down my first cup. Thea made me late; I had some catching up to do. It was justifiable at the time.

Beckett, a half-second behind because he was still too focused on the dumb hat, set his cup down on the counter and wiped the red from his lips. He still hadn't quite learned how to shave properly, so they had stubbles of hair to grip onto. I couldn't help but laugh.

"What is it this time, Carter? Something in my teeth?" he asked, already picking at them before I could answer. It didn't matter, I didn't get to answer anyway. To this day, I'm unsure what I would've said. I couldn't admit that I'd been staring at his lips, after all.

Eddie had burst into the kitchen, Thea's arm slung across his shoulder, the two of them singing god knows what with their undistinguishably slurred lyrics. He was the first to stop, shushing Thea for a moment before she quieted down and he yelled, "It's time for a drinking game, you and Beckett, me and Thea, let's go!"

And I wish I could tell you what followed was an admirable display of dexterity from the two most sober people at the party against the two most intoxicated. But no, I can't. Eddie chose the game and, of course, he chose strip beer pong. Why I had expected any less from the guy who told me theatre kids weren't friends until they'd helped one another out of costume is beyond me. Beckett and I, while logically capable of winning this game, were utterly destroyed. Eddie and Thea were gracious enough to call the game once we were left with only underwear, which I made sure to thank them for later, regardless of if they remembered doing so or not.

He and I may have started the game as the soberest people at the party, but we did not end it that way. Beckett was, despite his many faults, a gentleman and took as many of the cups as he could handle before subjecting me to such torment, but even I couldn't say I was necessarily seeing straight. Once the victors had thoroughly gloated and celebrated their triumph with yet more alcohol, Beckett and I were allowed to clothe ourselves once again. Most of what happened after that remains hazy to me, though there are two scenes from that night I remember with a surprising amount of detail.

I remember Victor and Valerie finally making an appearance, crying out that another game was necessary since they had missed the first. A three-way game of strip beer pong was just too much for our inebriated minds to fathom at that moment in time so suggestions were taken for what we would do. And, of course, I was outvoted five to one for the riveting game of, you guessed it, truth or dare.

Personally, I saw no point in the game as, knowing them, it was just going to be a game worthier of the name dare or drink because they deemed anyone lame enough to take truth was simply not quite drunk enough yet. The game went on as expected, especially considering the number of horny theatre teens in the room. A lot of "make-out with this or that person" dares, one, in particular, standing out.

"Dare," Thea half said, half slurred, hanging off the couch, upside down. It was her favorite way of sitting, regardless of her mental state, so at least it was comforting to see she remained mostly herself.

"Hmm…let me think…Thea, I dare you…to make Jaea a reality! Or is it Thane? Whatever, I dare you to kiss Jane," Valerie chuckled and everyone, as per usual, sounded out in a choir of mocking oohs.

"Ah, well, Jane, what do you say?" she asked, turning her head to face me.

As I was leaning against the arm of the couch, sat on the floor, we were already face to face. I couldn't help but laugh and shot a glance at Eddie. "Well, I've already kissed one of the gang. May as well work towards completing the full set."

"You sure?" Thea mouthed as everyone laughed and I heard Valerie mumbling something about how she'd kill me if I tried coming for Victor.

I simply shrugged, cupped her cheek in one hand, and gave her a quick peck on the lips. With her hanging upside down, it made me chuckle softly because it was almost like she was Spider-Man, and I was Mary Jane. A strange thought, I'll admit, to have while sharing a kiss with your best friend, but I still find it amusing.

The choir of oohs, as to be expected, returned with a vengeance as I leaned back against the couch once more. Thea, flushed from being drunk as a skunk, giggled and booped my nose. "Two down, three to go," she grinned.

"Three?" I tilted my head.

She tilted hers towards Beckett, who by now had lost his flannel. I was glad we weren't matching anymore, it's not like I needed any more fuel to be added to everyone's fire when it came to insisting, we'd be a good fit.

I rolled my eyes, or at least I think I did. I was sobering up by this point, after all.

"C'mon now, truth or dare…Jane?" Thea had a wide smile across her lips.

I, not nearly as amused, shot don't-you-dare daggers at her with my eyes. She just kept grinning and eventually, I gave in. "Dare." I slumped back against the couch and awaited whatever horrible fate she had decided upon for me.

"Jane, my dear, I dare you…to go spend some alone time with Beckett."

My glare intensified to a degree that seemed beyond impossible.

"Sounds like seven minutes in heaven to me, folks," Eddie grinned.

Victor and Valerie gave whoops and hollers in agreement.

"As much as I loved our Jaea-Thane detour, this sounds like just what the love doctor ordered!" Valerie said, snuggling into Victor. His arm adjusted around her shoulders. Even I'm not cynical enough to say they didn't look picture perfect in that moment. "What do you say, lover boy?" All their eyes were on Beckett by this point, as I'd received the dare and had no say in the matter, but he certainly still did. I was counting on him saying no.

"I mean, why not?" he chuckled and hiccupped, rubbing the back of his neck and avoiding their gazes. At least he seemed to feel as awkward about it all as I did. Next thing the two of us knew, we were shoved into a coat closet with only the light of a cell phone timer, which was set to alert us when our sentencing in hell was over.

We stayed silent for about the first minute.

"Well…this is awkward," Beckett laughed slightly.

"No kidding," I huffed, blowing a strand of hair out of my face, "Why'd you even agree to it? You could've just said no and then we wouldn't be stuck in here." I couldn't even look at him. We were both sitting with our knees tucked to our chests and, even then, we were still way too close. Despite the two layers of clothes separating our skin, my knees felt bare against his.

"Well, I figured they would just come up with something shittier to make you do, and this really isn't that bad in the grand scheme of things," he said with the light of the timer illuminating his face, so I saw him raise his brow in a cocky, you-know-I'm-right kind of way.

I didn't respond, just shifted my gaze away from him.

"So, what's the plan, Carter? Sitting here in silence for the next..." he looked at the timer, "five minutes and thirty-two seconds? Thirty-one seconds? Thirty seconds?"

"Definitely don't need the play-by-play, Bucket," I groaned.

"Alright, then give me something better to do," he offered.

"Like what?"

"Oh, I dunno, talking is better than silence though."

Silence followed, about thirty seconds of it, before I spoke up again, "Look, I appreciate you agreeing to this. They certainly could've made me do something even more embarrassing, knowing how creative they get when they drink."

Beckett chuckled and the light from the timer caught in his eyes. "I'm sure they could've. I'm surprised no one's had to streak yet."

"Shush, don't go giving them any ideas," I half-said, half-laughed. He laughed too and his hiccup led us into another period of silence. My gaze remained on the floor for a short bit before I raised it only to accidentally meet his gaze and drop it again.

"What's wrong? They're just eyes, you can look at them," he chuckled.

"It'd be weird, just sitting here in the dark staring into each other's eyes. Either too romantic or too murder-esque for my taste," I said and shook my head.

"Well, I guess that makes sense. They say the soul's in the eyes, after all, it'd be weird to be looking at each other's souls, that's personal shit after all," he laughed. He must've been less sober than I thought. "I guess you'll just never see what my soul's doing right now then."

"What does that even mean?" He'd piqued my interest, so I looked up and met his gaze. He'd crossed his eyes and was making the most ridiculous of faces. I, regrettably, snorted in laughter.

"Ha! Did I just—did I just get you to snort? The calm, cool, constantly collected Jane Carter to *snort*? How undignified!" Beckett laughed and beamed triumphantly, the gleam in his eyes keeping my gaze until I noticed that they were different colors. The right was blue, the left green. How had I not noticed before? How could so many points of interest culminate in one face I'd deemed so ordinary?

As he laughed and I rethought everything, the timer buzzed, and our sentence was lived out. We were officially free to collect our belongings and assimilate into the world once more, though who knew if we would be successful.

Thea flung open the door to the closet and the light nearly blinded us. He crawled out first and found a nice spot on the living room rug to sprawl out on. I took my place back at the arm of the couch and sighed softly as we were badgered with questions.

Life moved forward, outside of those four tight walls, though I'm not quite sure how the rest of the night went. All I really remember is waking up that next morning and noticing that the buttons on my flannel had swapped sides.

CHAPTER 7

Choosing Wisely

You know, I thought I'd have left scantrons in the past along with the manila-colored desks with impossibly uncomfortable chairs and the ridiculous time-wasting movie days we'd have when teachers were just tired of teaching. Oddly enough, only one of those was left behind me, which I will not complain about as the padded chairs make a movie day much easier to sleep through. The fact that after the movie, I woke up to that familiar sheet of paper with the words "Pop Quiz" across the top, however, was far less welcome. It probably would have been easier if I'd still be sat in one of those torturously stiff chairs because then at least I might've watched a bit of the movie between my trips to the clouds and gotten a couple points. Instead, I was left with a series of meaningless and unanswerable questions, just as I always seemed to be as of late.

It was easy, this time around because I didn't have enough information to debate anything. Marking C all the way down and marching out of the class was the best I could do. Sometimes it's better that way, no information because at least I looked confident while doing it. I don't think I'd ever made a confident choice before that. I had people to do that for me. There was always some shred of doubt in the back of my mind, even for the most trivial of things.

When I returned to my dorm, I was met with an empty room. It was a surprise, but a welcome one. I didn't want to have the awkward yet conventional roommate small talk that always followed me returning from class. Really, all I wanted to do was sit in bed and watch pointless videos as wasting time watching something I'd chosen would be a nice change of pace from that hellhole of a GE.

Just as I'd gotten comfortable, however, I got an email notification from the TA, the Beelzebub of said hellhole. Grades for the quizzes had already been posted. Staring at the perfect score in my grade book, I couldn't help but laugh. There had been times in my life when my indecision paralyzed me, but not during that quiz. No, it wasn't the seemingly important decisions that troubled me, but the minor ones, the ones that my prior life, my high school life, was chock full of.

～

"Jane, c'mon, just pick already. We've gotta get going," Thea tugged on the sleeve of my coat, my other hand resting on the glass of the pastry case of Roast with the Most, much to a certain barista boy's dismay.

"You don't need to rush but could you at least take your hand off the glass? I just wiped it down and now I'm going to have to clean away all the fingerprints you're making," Beckett rubbed the back of his neck.

"It's a big decision, T. This is going to have to hold me over until lunch, after all," I said, still pondering over pastries. My mind was torn between a cinnamon raisin bagel and a chocolate croissant. My heart cried out for chocolate, but my stomach demanded the sustainable energy the bagel would provide. But what to choose?

"Why don't you get both?" Beckett finally chimed in, "The two sides of this debate seem unswayable."

"Here we go," Thea sighed and sank to the floor.

"Okay, look, even if that was a good suggestion in theory, do you not realize how quickly that sort of flawed logic falls apart? The best part about a bagel is the crunch after it's been toasted and the way the cream cheese melts a little. A chocolate croissant is dependent on the heat to keep it molten, and the flakiness vanishes the second the thing starts to cool. If I get both, whichever I eat first is going to be great but whatever I save will just be sad and damp." I paced along the side of the case as I made mine.

Beckett chuckled at my plight and Thea was anything but amused. She's lived through this debate and others like it time and time again.

"Okay, you want the croissant. Let's go, we're already late." Thea groaned as she stood up, leaning her whole weight against my back as if to pressure me into speeding up my decision-making process.

"Fine, fine. A cinnamon raisin bagel with cream cheese, toasted, please. And quit acting like that's my fault. You're the one who kept me waiting outside for half an hour while you fixed your hair," I countered as I set my payment in the sweaty palm of the guy behind the counter. I pulled my hand away as soon as physically possible.

"Coming right up. Where are you guys headed in such a hurry anyway? Saturdays are usually reserved for hanging around Roast for you two," Beckett said, finishing up my pre-ordered Smokin' Hot Brocklate, aptly named after one of Thea's past summer crushes. It was his calves, she said, so toned from soccer, that really got her. The drink was nothing more than glorified hot chocolate, in which a mix of house toasted white chocolate and smoked dark chocolate was melted into steamed milk and topped with, guess what, smoke-infused whipped cream. So much work for such a staple of a café beverage.

"We're headed to weekend rehearsals. We got a little behind on everything, so Mitchell suggested this or an extra hour after school for the next few weeks. This was a no-brainer," Thea mumbled, pretending to be dying it seemed.

"Sounds like the rock of the rock and the hard place," he sprinkled chocolate shavings on top of the whipped cream. It's not like they mattered, hidden underneath the lid.

"Is that the better choice?" Thea pulled her lips back just slightly and furrowed her brows, unsure.

"It better be." He held out the finished drink to me and, as my hand wrapped around the cardboard sleeve of the cup, our eyes met. For some reason unknown to me, he was smiling in his crooked way, his lone dimple carved deep in his speckled granite cheek.

"Watch out, you might get stuck like that." I regretted that the corner of my lip raised even slightly as I said those words. I didn't need him getting too used to that.

"Yeah, yeah," he waved a hand as he popped my bagel out of the toaster and put, surprisingly, the correct amount of cream cheese on it before stuffing it into a little paper bag and giving it a gently toss in my direction.

For once, my reflexes didn't let me down and upon catching the bag I was tugged to the door by an overly over-it Thea. "Catch you two later," Beckett called after us and tilted his visor in our direction.

"See you, Beck!" Thea called back as I simply raised my drink, not bothering to look back. I was sure he was wearing that same goofy grin so there was no reason to get another look at it.

Thea shot me a look the second we got to the car; I could feel it in my bones as I struggled to tug my snagging keys out of my coat pocket.

"What?" I asked as I unlocked the car and sunk into the driver's seat, setting my Smokin' Hot Brocklate in the cupholder and the bagel bag beside it so it'd stay warm as I drove. And yes, I know eating while driving isn't illegal, but I've always preferred to keep two hands on the wheel.

"Oh c'mon? We're not going to talk about the fact that I needed a welding mask to watch the two of you. Sparks were flying," Thea said, kicking on the seat warmers because she always seems to be cold.

"Stop being so dramatic," I rolled my eyes as I pulled out of my usual parking space and headed to school. Thea, knowing me better than I know myself sometimes, took out the bagel and held it to my mouth for me to take a bite while I drove.

"I'm not the one who needs someone to feed them as they drive," Thea said, lowering her hand as I chewed.

"Fair point but the only sparks you saw must have been a result of your failing vision. Jeez, what's it like to be going blind?" I asked through a mouthful of half-chewed bagel.

"And I'm the dramatic one." She groaned and rolled her eyes but obliged once I motioned for another bite. "You don't even think he's a little cute? He's totally into you."

"That's just one of our bits, you know that." I would've waved her off but both hands were on the wheel. "We'd never actually work."

"Why not?"

"Well for starters, he—" She kind of stumped me with that one. I'd never really thought about why we wouldn't work; I just knew that the fact we wouldn't was set in stone. I eventually settled on some form of loose reasoning. "He's Bucket." With that, I nodded wholeheartedly, as if what I said was indisputable.

"What is that even supposed to mean? He's cute and he clearly likes you!"

I didn't respond, just motioned for another bite.

Thea groaned and slumped.

I took the last bite as I pulled into the back lot of our school, putting an end to her onslaught of what-ifs and why-nots. "Let's go, we're already late."

As she and I tugged on the, surprisingly locked, door to the theatre department, a sleepless Eddie slung an arm around each of our shoulders. "Locked? Not surprising. Mitchell's never been one for weekend timeliness. Good news is, he's likely picking up donuts. Thea, got a bobby pin?"

Thea shook her head, "Out of luck."

"I've got one!" chimed a swiftly approaching Valerie with Victor by her side. She held it up for all the world to see.

"A true lifesaver, as always," Eddie grinned as he swiped the pin, bent it, and proceeded to pick the lock of the theatre door.

I stood, shocked, as nobody protested. Was this a normal occurrence? Just breaking into school property without even considering the repercussions? I, however, was not about to argue as the daily dose of rain was just starting to fall. Rather than end up soaked, I allowed Eddie to finish showing off his rather questionable talent and filed into the back of the theatre with the others. I took sips of my Smokin' Hot Brocklate in between Thea's spurts of requesting to hold the cup to warm her hands and the greeting of fellow thespians making their way into the warm and dry, yet strictly off limits, supervisorless theatre.

"Twenty minutes? Line at Donut Think About It must be pretty long today," Eddie chuckled. Everyone laughed along, seemingly knowing the drill while I was left in the dark. "Should we just get things going? Thea, thoughts? You're directing after all."

Everyone turned to look at her and she nearly fell off the desk she was sitting on, fumbling with my drink and her hand warmer. "M-Me?" she flushed, shifting from printer paper white to stop light red in the blink of an eye. For someone who loved to be in control, she sure seemed awkward whenever it was freely handed to her.

"Well yeah, it makes the most sense for you to be the one bossing us around. It's either you or Val and I think we'd all prefer you," Victor chimed in and nudged Valerie's side for good measure. I worried for a moment that this would be another one of their spontaneous break-ups but, luckily, she seemed to take the jab in a more gracious manner.

"Okay, um, well, I guess the crew could start finalizing the backdrop. You said there was a lot of detail work to do, right Val?"

"Oh yeah, too much maybe. I'm not sure we'll get it done today. You and Mitchell were really specific on how above and beyond you wanted it to be, after all," she said, sitting up so she was no longer leaning against Victor's shoulder.

"Hm, well, if tech's working on lighting and sound queues for… Act 2 all scenes," Thea hesitated and waited for an assuring nod from Victor before continuing, "Some of the cast could give you guys in the crew a hand with the painting? I'd say we save the bigger scenes for whenever it is Mitchell shows up so Jane and Eddie could be some extra manpower. Think they'll be enough to speed things up a bit?"

"Two extra sets of hands are more than I could've asked for. How do you guys feel about getting a little messy?" Valerie grinned.

"You know I'm always ready for a good time," Eddie leapt off his respective desk.

They all turned to me, and I shrugged, offering a small smile, "It would be nice to get a better look at how everything comes together."

"That's the spirit!" Eddie gripped my hands and tugged me up and back to the workshop while I silently said a goodbye to my Smokin' Hot Brocklate. I hope Thea finished off the beverage that I never got to but knowing her she probably held it until it was cold and tossed it once it no longer served its purpose. What a waste.

I stumbled after Eddie, used to being dragged around in my friend group enough to not trip like I used to. Valerie was going on and on about the need for perfection, no mistakes, no slip-ups, all that jazz. I was listening but I think Eddie was more excited about the possible prospect of finger-painting to care much about the instructions. "Got it?" she asked, hoping to affirm that we understood and get us to ask questions if we didn't. I nodded as I actually did understand, and Eddie bellowed a cheerful yep.

With that, Valerie tossed us each a smock and a brush, wanting us to fill in the taped-out bricks with varying shades of beige while she was taping out the rest of the bricks and background details. Others were busy building set pieces, making the pounding of hammers on nails a prevalent bit of surrounding noise while also making it clear how much work Valerie had to do on her own. Not one but three backdrops was a grand demand for a group, let alone an individual. Especially since each section had to line up, set apart on rotating triangular pillars, which I later learned were called Periaktos in case you were wondering, that made scenery changes easy to accomplish mid-show when the lights were dropped but the creation of said scenery was anything but.

Eddie was doing a free for all of beige tones on each brick. I, on the other hand, was planning out each brick perfectly, making sure it wouldn't come in direct contact with a brick of the same shade of beige. While my methodology was bound to be more aesthetically pleasing, Eddie's method seemed more, well, fun. Whenever I stole a glance in his direction, he was throwing paint at the white rectangles, not caring if there was a bit of splashing or bleeding over.

Our sides weren't going to match at all.

"What's up? Why'd you stop?" he asked, grinning even though he was splattered in shades of beige. Speckles of it even shone in his curls like light through autumn leaves.

"Don't you think you should be a little more careful?" I arched a brow.

"Aw c'mon, this is more fun!" Unarguably true, yes, but not what we were tasked with.

I rolled my eyes and continued with my method. While his was messy, it was fast, as he was up on the ladder to get the higher blocks before I'd finished half of my lower section. Every brick was a bagel or a croissant, ironically enough beige themselves, but this time I didn't have Thea to just make the choice for me. It rested all on my shoulders and Valerie, with her let's call them particularities, was not someone I wanted to disappoint.

"What's taking you so long, slowpoke?" Eddie practically sang the words. I could tell he liked to seem better than me at something but really, he was just faster at making a mess.

"There's nothing wrong with taking time to actually plan things out," I huffed, blowing a strand of hair out of my eyes, and continuing to paint blocks beige.

"Okay, well, I've finished my part so why don't I give you a hand with yours," he said with a hint of triumph in his voice. In an act of what I'll sum up as reckless bravado, he leaped off the ladder but took it to the ground with him. It and the can of green paint that was resting atop it. I gasped, he turned around, but neither of us could stop the paint from tumbling atop the pillar and oozing down Eddie's wall of beige bricks like blood in a horror movie, trauma and terror included.

"Look what you did!" I ran a hand through my hair, not caring that the paint in my hands left me with near-blonde roots until my next shower.

"I didn't mean to! Shit, what are we gonna do?" he went to try to wipe the paint off the pillar, but I grabbed hold of his wrist.

"You're just going to smear it if you do that," I took a deep breath and prompted him to do so as well, "Okay, okay, we can fix this, yeah? We just have to *think*." I emphasized the word to make sure he heard me. A quick and ill-thought-out decision wasn't what we needed, we needed to rationalize.

"How are we going to fix this? There's green lines running down this whole thing!" Eddie rubbed his hands together as he whisper-yelled, as even he was smart enough to keep Valerie from hearing of our screw-up. Yes, our, because whether I liked it or not, I would've taken the blame with him. No man left behind or some bullshit like that, y'know?

"It's fine, we'll figure something out. I'll make sure Val doesn't see what happened, alright? You just go grab The—" I hesitated. She already had enough on her plate. She didn't need this on top of everything, a mistake made by the two people she trusted most not to mess up. We'd handle this. "Go grab some more paint."

"What color?" Eddie asked, puzzled.

I gazed at the wall for a few moments. Once it was in my head, the idea took control of my lips and made their corners raise. "Green."

***

Once I felt Eddie had a solid grasp of the plan and no intention to stray from it, I went off to distract Valerie. Lucky for us, she'd moved on from backdrop planning to prop design. I found her putting together fake flower arrangements while simultaneously staining a newly built table. It's like she had more than two hands, all the work she was doing.

"Hey, done with the bricks?"

And more than two eyes. I wasn't even in her line of sight. I thought up a quick lie. "No, no, not yet. I finished my half but Eddie's still working on his. Figured I should come help you?"

"The more the merrier," she tossed me the rag she'd been using on the table, "What do you think? Red roses and yellow geraniums or yellow roses and red geraniums? It's important. If the flowers are off, it'll be distracting to the audience and then they won't be paying attention to the actors and all they'll think about is how the flowers were so off. Don't even get me started on if we should use baby's breath or feverfew daisies to balance them out. What do you think?" she held two clumps of fake flowers out to me in each hand.

All I could think was "Was that what I sounded like?"

"Uh, I dunno, maybe yellow with red?

"Maybe? We need solid decisions here, Jane. C'mon, get with the program," she threw up her arms and sank down into one of the plastic chairs nearby. She wasn't even cast, and she was over the top, I still couldn't understand these people.

"Yellow with red. Definitely," I said, trying to make my work with the rag look confident so my answer would sound even better. "How could you even debate red and yellow?"

After a moment or two of pondering, she nodded in agreement, tossing the red and yellow combination over her shoulder in disdain, "You're right, what was I thinking?" She was really proving that she belonged here. "But now it's down to baby's breath or feverfew daisies!" She flung her arms and head back, looking limp in the chair.

"Just pick whichever one you think would be best," I shrugged a shoulder, instantly regretting my answer. I sounded like Thea. Or worse, Beckett.

"Just pick whichever one I think would be best? This isn't some circus sideshow, Jane. Some of us want this to look good on college apps and how is it going to look good on college apps when I can't even get the flower arrangements right?" She was standing now, pacing around the table, and making all kinds of wild hand motions. I was surprised smoke wasn't coming out of her ears, what with her mind going a million miles a minute after all.

"They're never going to hear about the flower arrangements if you never make them," I said simply, tossing the rag over my shoulder when I'd finished staining the table and leaning against a cabinet that was likely full of paints and stains and polishes galore. Probably organized in alphabetical order too, with how Valerie likes to keep her work environment.

"Well…yeah…but…" she stammered, stopping in her tracks. I had her.

"Just make a choice. Can't be that hard for someone as experienced as yourself." Flattery never hurts.

"I…you're right. Baby's breath it is." And with that, she was stuffing flowers into vases.

I wasn't entirely sure if she was even listening at that point. She could've just as easily tuned me out and had a little internal debate to come up with an answer, just saying I was right because she saw my lips moving and didn't want me to think I was ignored. Well, I did, up until she spoke again.

"Thanks," she smiled slightly. In that moment, I was sure she'd heard me. I'd completely forgotten about the bricks and the beige until Eddie came over, not a speck of green on his clothes or skin. Guess he must've been careful that time around.

"Hey, the walls are finished if you'd like to take a look," he rubbed his hands together, a nervous habit of his I'd picked up on.

"Oh great!" Valerie said, setting the flowers down, "That's one more thing off the list." We followed him back over to the sight of the once-calamity. Valerie was the first to make a sound. Upon sight, she gasped.

"What did you do?!"

We winced.

"It looks…amazing!" she turned to us, beaming. Eddie was the first to start breathing again while I took another moment to convince, even though she was right. It looked, well, like it was meant to. The green paint streaks became ivy vines under Eddie's surprisingly careful hand. The leaves looked like they were ready to catch the rain, feel the sun, and move if a gust were to come by. He somehow pulled it off and I think he was the most awestruck of us all. "Where did you two get the idea for this? Jane, this must've been you!"

"Actually, it was all Eddie's idea." I gestured to him, offering a smile.

"Wha—" Before he could get the words out, Valerie threw her arms around him.

"Fantastic work! I can't believe how great this looks!" she practically sang before releasing him. "Great work, I'm amazed. You two take a break and see if Thea needs anything. If not, I'm sure I'll have something you can do." There was joy exuding in her steps as she walked off, likely to go debate more flowers.

Eddie waited until she was out of range to hear him whisper, "Why'd you do that?"

"Do what?" I feigned obliviousness, already headed toward the stage where Thea was likely running scenes with the rest of the cast.

"Why'd you tell her it was my idea? You're the one who came up with it," he jogged after me.

"You're the one who executed it. In a way that looked planned and purposeful." He cowered a bit in shame. "But, also, your side was better."

"Huh?"

"It turned out looking really cool, the splashed colors and chaos." I shrugged to prevent his head from getting too big.

It prevented nothing. "I knew it would," he grinned, stuffing his hands in his pockets.

"You couldn't have known how it'd look. You didn't have a plan," I countered, turning to him.

His eyes lit up. "Sometimes no plan is a plan."

~~~

Just as Eddie and I approached the stage, a loud and disheveled sounding voice called out, "Sorry I'm late, everyone!"
~~~

We all convened back in the classroom, eager to have some sort of structure to what was still a long day ahead. Even tech ran down the stair from their bat cave to come greet Mitchell, who, as predicted, had a donut box in each hand. "Good job on getting the door open, Eddie," he said.

Eddie chuckled, "Ah, you know it's nothing. Should just hurry up and get me a key already."

"You know I would if I could but alas district policy forbids it," our sopping wet supposed authority figure said as he set each box down on a desk and took off his coat. "What have I missed?"

Thea gave him a rundown of progress made and, at every word, he seemed impressed. He could tell she was handling being in charge just fine, at least for the most part. Eddie and I were sure to leave our blunder out of the summary, instead saying that backdrop one was finished and drying while the other two had minor details left to rehash.

"Flower arrangements have been decided upon and made," Valerie chimed in.

"That's a full two weeks ahead of schedule," Mitchell said, stunned. I wanted to be sure he was joking but couldn't be. It seemed perfectly accurate for her to be capable of spending two weeks debating red and yellow or yellow and red. "How'd that happen?"

"I had some help," she shot me a quick smile.

"Well, in that case, I think everyone's deserving of a break. Have at 'em." He waved a hand at the pink boxes, and they were attacked with ravenous fervor. By the time I got to them, there were only two donuts left.

A maple bar or chocolate with sprinkles? They both had their pros and cons, which I was ready to debate until Thea came up behind me and snagged the chocolate.

"Cheers," she grinned, holding her donut out to me.

Picking up the bar and clinking donuts with her, I sighed a breath of relief. Baby steps.

CHAPTER 8

Movie Misfits

I feel some may say it's odd I have yet to speak of romance, with the environment of a university being so, well, out there. But, sorry to quench the burning question, no, college has not been the glowing garden of Venus everyone claims it to be, at least not yet and not for me. But I can't say it couldn't have been. There were a few instances from which a romance could have blossomed, surely, but it was simply against my best interest so out came the weed killer in each case.

It's not like I haven't thought about letting it happen, seeing where the wind takes me. I have, I'm just not much the romantic type. I'd never dreamed of my wedding as a kid, never picked out dresses or décor. That was more T than me. She was the one of us I could envision getting married, at least, but me, not so much. I saw myself as a cool wine- or a crazy cat-aunt more than anything. Maybe I'd find someone, but I doubted it. I am better at pushing people away and a change in environment has done little to change this habit but that can't be a surprise at this point. I've never even been on a date, at least, not in the traditional sense. My first was…unconventional and unintentional, let's say.

I was, for the millionth time that week, lost in a world of doodles in my dreadful AP World History class. The slamming of textbooks on my desk startled me back down into the map-covered classroom.

"There she is! Was worried we lost you forever," Thea grinned, resting her elbows on the very textbooks with which I was audibly attacked, "Well, were you anywhere interesting?"

"Just in the clouds," I said, closing my notebook and stuffing it into my bag.

"No kidding, the bell rang a good fifteen minutes ago, and here you are, still in class," she said, picking up the pencils her books knocked off my desk.

I rolled my eyes in disbelief and in doing so got a good look around at the sea of empty desks and at the clock I normally stared intensely at throughout all of Ms. Carlson's dreadful lectures. "Oh shit, you're not kidding!"

"Nope, I'm not, meaning you're late to rehearsal, chop-chop," Thea clapped her hands together as she walked over to the door and held it for me as I ran out, still stuffing away my pencil pouch. "That's the kind of hustle I'm looking for!" she chuckled as she ran after me.

As I crashed through the door and stuttered out an apology, I received a resentful wave to the side from Mitchell and knew I needed to get my corset on and my ass on the stage. Thea, being the gracious friend and dearest director that she was, laced me up and sent me on my way.

Eddie greeted me with a bow. "Glad you could find time in your busy schedule to join us."

I rolled my eyes and got right into it, something for which Mitchell was grateful, as I'd clearly wasted enough of his time. The man was a hypocrite but he was in charge so what could I do but put up with his tardy policy hypocrisy?

Rehearsal went fine, as it normally did, with the only hiccups being Eddie's insistence on the occasionally ad-libbed line to keep things fresh and me on my toes. Was it entertaining? Yes, of course. Was it time-consuming and at least a bit bothersome to work around? Absolutely.

But somehow, someway, we ended up making it through the day and only having to rerun the scenes Eddie intentionally screwed up. After we were dismissed and I finally got to pull off that horrible torture device of a corset, Mitchell called me back to his office.

"Is everything alright?" he asked, not bothering to look up from the script as he scribbled notes into its well-worn pages.

I was a little stunned, so I hesitated before speaking up. "Hm? Yeah? Why wouldn't I be?"

"You were late. You're never late." This time he looked up.

I told him I just zoned out a bit in class, but he didn't seem to buy it. He looked in my eyes for a while, almost an awkward amount of time before speaking up again and putting a halt to a seemingly endless silence.

"You're worn out. Overworked. Have you done anything besides schoolwork and this? Anything where the main topic of conversation wasn't this production or anything that goes into it?" he said after lowering his gaze back to the script.

I opened my mouth to speak, to protest, but couldn't bring myself to lie. It was true, every single conversation I'd had since "auditioning" was about the show. When we all went to the coffee shop, it was the only topic of conversation. Even treehouse chats with Thea were all about what I should do, questions I had, how exciting opening night would be, the latter of which was her trying to convince me. I wasn't sold on it having the potential to be "life-changing" and "the best night of my young life" quite yet. She was adamant. I was apprehensive. Our usual.

"That's what I thought. Friday's canceled. Now, I'm begging you, go have some actual fun before you lose your mind and leave here in a straitjacket and me looking for a new lead," Mitchell lowered the script just enough so I could see his eyes, "Understood?" He didn't allow me to respond. "Great. Now go make plans with the eavesdroppers." He nodded to the door, silently and near-motionlessly ushering me out of his office.

I almost hit Eddie in the face with the door on my way out he'd been so close to it.

He, alongside Thea, Victor, and Valerie, clapped and hollered. "Your first round of pre-show exhaustion is a big deal, y'know?" he grinned as he patted me on the back.

I blinked, still a bit confused by everything that had happened.

"Don't worry, we've all been there," Valerie said.

Victor, of course, chimed in. "It's true. Some of us more than others." The group collectively turned to Thea. I, having known her for years, was not surprised at this reveal. Imagining her overworking herself to the point of exhaustion was as easy as imagining her as blonde or bubbly. It's not exactly hard to imagine reality, after all.

"Hey, what're you guys looking at me for?" she gasped incredulously, looking around at everyone wearing the same expression a kicked puppy would have donned.

Eddie shifts from my side to wrap his arms around her from behind and rest his chin atop her head. "Really? Don't feign innocence T, bullshit's not a good look on you. You may not be an actor but you're the biggest drama queen in this joint. And that's coming from me."

"Oh c'mon, that's not true!" Thea squirmed out of his grasp; her alabaster cheeks flushed red in embarrassment. I couldn't help but laugh as they all tried to comfort her and let her down easy. She was high strung, and anyone wound up too tight was bound to snap more often than someone who was, well, not. Someone like me.

"Thea, you're more wound up than a jack-in-the-box but it's a lot scarier when you pop," Valerie chuckles. Admittedly, a dumb joke. But did I still laugh? Yes, yes, I did. "But for once, it's not you. It's Jane's first freak-out Friday. This is cause for celebration."

"Indeed," Eddie agreed and turned to me, resting his elbows on a desk with his head in his clasped hands while batting his eyelashes, "Jane darling, what would you like to do for your mandatory day of free-from-rehearsals fun?"

"Can we hold that thought? Weren't we supposed to go to the Roast? We called in our order thirty minutes ago guys," Victor finally pulled his head out of the clouds. I figured his look of searching was just his normal spaced-out face but for once he had, to the others, an actual point.

"Oh shit, you're right!" Eddie noticed my confused look, "You were with Mitchell. I ordered you a Karen, you looked like you needed it. C'mon everyone, let's go, we can brainstorm there." He ushered us out of the theatre and towards the parking lot. I was happy for the change of scenery and, quite frankly, in desperate need of a coffee, so I was more than willing to drive everyone upon being voluntold to do so.

The short drive to the Roast was spent mostly with Thea and Eddie arguing with Victor and Valerie over which pair should have control of the music. I didn't mind much either way, but each was adamantly against the other. By the time they had all agreed on a song and Eddie had plugged his phone into the aux, I was already pulling into my usual parking space. Equally as unsurprisingly, I was forced to sit and listen as they quelled their previous aggression and belted out, of course, Dancing Queen by ABBA. Were theatre geeks even allowed to listen to other music?

The mophead behind the counter whipped around when the bell above the door chimed. "Finally, you guys really took your sweet time getting here," Beckett said and carried our tray of drinks to our usual spot at the beyond antique velvet couch and its surrounding, not quite matching armchairs. Eddie paid for everyone, ignoring our protests.

"No, no, this is my treat. We're celebrating, after all," he said as he signed the receipt.

"Oh, what's the occasion?" Beckett asked as he hung up his apron and visor, clocking off for the day. We all knew he really should have gotten off forty minutes ago but wanted to make sure we got our drinks. Not that he'd never admit that. He plopped down in the free armchair, the other occupied by Victor with Valerie perched on one of the arms. The two looked something like a 1950's mobsters' couple.

"Tomorrow will mark our first Friday free from rehearsal and it's all thanks to Jane having a minor meltdown," Thea stated matter-of-factly, having comfortably sprawled out on the couch so her legs were across my lap and her head was in Eddie's.

"There was no meltdown," I corrected, shrugging as I took a sip of my both, way-too-strong and somehow just-strong-enough coffee "Mitchell just said I seemed off and needed a day without theatre to get my head back in it is all."

"Either way, it's a day off so we've got to do something. We'll never get this type of free time again." Eddie was playing with Thea's hair with one hand as he spoke, with the other resting just behind his head.

"Since you're the one who got us the day off, you have to decide what we do with it," Victor tossed the wadded-up wrapper to his straw at me. It bounced off my forehead.

"Do I really have to be the one to decide? Besides, it's a day off, don't you think we should, oh I don't know, not just hang out together like we would if it weren't a day off?"

They looked at me like I had three eyes.

"Are you saying you're sick and tired of us? Already? What a fool I was for thinking you could tough it out a little longer than this." Eddie smacked his forehead and looked to the heavens as we laughed. Beckett joined in after a moment, always a beat behind.

I rolled my eyes and tossed Victor's wadded straw wrapper in his direction but missed. Eddie threw up his hands, "Not only are you sick of me, but now you're attacking me? The betrayal!" Thea almost spat out her drink at his near shriek of a tone.

"Oh hush," I laughed, slightly awkwardly as some of the other customers—the usual crowd of unwashed hipsters, and unhinged screenwriters—looked over. I knew it wasn't like my friends to care, though, so their antics continued.

"We all knew this day would come: the day Jane decided she was through with our bullshit, so, she up and left us," Valerie threw her head back in anguish, the back of her palm pressed against her forehead while her other hand clutched her heart. I knew she was being dramatic, but I couldn't help but wonder if that was really something they'd been preparing for.

Victor proceeded to clutch his own chest as if he'd been shot and sink down in the chair in mock woe.

Thea pinched the bridge of her nose as she held back false tears. "I could've seen this coming from any of them, but you?"

With all eyes on us, Beckett could do nothing but laugh his ass off and be just as little help as ever.

"Okay, okay, I'm sorry I even suggested it," I chuckled as I ran a hand through my hair, trying not to let my nerves burn through my cheeks.

"That's the spirit," Eddie grinned, "Got a plan yet?"

"Um…" I thought for a moment, "We could go to a movie?"

Beckett cleared his throat, "Really? You're going to take your day off from theatre…and go to a theatre?"

"*We're* going to a theatre, you're coming after all, right?" Valerie asked, teasing as she added, "You wouldn't have Jane stuck as a fifth wheel, would you?" They all had a good laugh at the one.

Eddie pretended to wipe tears from his eyes. "Oh please, if anyone's the fifth wheel here it's me. Though I wouldn't protest to you giving me some company." He shot a wink and blew a kiss to Beckett but couldn't keep a straight face and broke into a fit of laughter.

"Well, I've got the afternoon free tomorrow and no plans, so I don't see why not," he chuckled and shrugged a shoulder as his thumbs traced the rim of his coffee cup.

"Alright, so it's settled. We're seeing a movie," Victor nodded once.

"But there's still so much left to settle!" Valerie exclaimed, "Are we going to get food? Will we do that before or after the movie? Which movie do we want to see? What are the showtimes of said movie? This is so far from settled, I wouldn't even call it a plan!"

"Well, what movies are even out?" Beckett asked and sparked the second debate of the day. The group split itself into teams, horror flick versus romantic comedy, I'll leave it to you to guess who was on what team. This time, the underdog group, whose mantra was I don't really care either way just somebody make a decision, that was comprised normally of just me had a new member join the ranks.

"Do they always decide on plans like this?" Beckett leaned passed the edge of his chair to make his words easier heard over the shouting match.

"How could you even say we'd all enjoy that as a group? Everyone knows you two are just going to make out through the whole thing!" Eddie's voice echoes off the walls of the coffee shop, which had been getting gradually less and less occupied since our arrival.

"Yeah, just about," I leaned towards Beckett as their voices got louder.

"What, you got a problem with horror films or something? Too scared?" Valerie snapped.

"We just don't want to see that plotless drivel!" Thea countered, throwing her arms in the air in exasperation. In doing so, she managed to nail Eddie right in the jaw. The shouting match was put on pause for a fit of laughter from all involved parties.

I groaned, shaking my head. "See? This is what happens when you guys argue! Someone always ends up getting hurt, feelings usually but sometimes physically. If this is a so-called celebration of me getting us a day off, shouldn't I be the one picking the movie?"

They all opened their mouths to speak, shut them wordlessly, exchanged glances, and looked down in shame in a perfectly choreographed way. "You're right, it's your choice what kind of movie we see," Thea twirled a strand of her hair around her finger.

"Thank you," I huffed and pondered for a moment or two. I had to decide something that would make everyone at least a little happy. I was drawing a blank.

"What about that one about the dystopian society centered around a video game? I think it's based on a book. I've heard it's got some jokes, a little bit of romance, and a bit of horror?" Beckett spoke up, shrugging with his hands up like a scale to weigh the pros and cons. "Seems like it's got a bit of something for everyone?"

He threw me a line and pulled me back in and, for that, I was grateful. "Oh yeah, I've been wanting to see that." I didn't even know what movie he was talking about. "We'll see that one. Everyone cool?"

After a few moments of silence and about four internal debates, the group mumbled their agreements and nodded their heads. Finally, after driving away every customer Roast had and nearly tearing apart our friend group, we made a decision.

"Okay, but we still haven't figured out where we're eating," Thea said as she sat up.

"Or, if we're eating," Valerie added, visibly perking up at the thought of another debate.

I groaned and Beckett turned to me, his mismatched eyes filled with a sense of knowing, practically screaming the words that barely managed to escape his lips before the bickering began.

"Here we go again."

〜〜

I knocked, loudly and ceaselessly, wondering what was taking her so long. "T, c'mon, we're going to be late…again! Mrs. Springer will probably kill me if I walk in late one more ti—" I fell into the doorway and into her as she swung it open. I felt the soft cushion of flannel as my cheek hit her shoulder and bright pinstripes assaulted my eyes.

"Why are you still in your pajamas, we're going to be so..." I stopped badgering her the second I saw her face. Paler than usual except for her Rudolph-reminiscent nose. She looked like hell.

"I'm sick, sorry J," she sniffled, and I took a few steps back.

"No kidding," I muttered, making sure to cover my mouth and turn my head so I didn't breathe in the cloud of illness that enveloped her. "I guess the movie's a bust, then?"

"No, no, you guys go, you need the break." She coughed, hacking up what seemed like both lungs. I grimaced but stepped inside, pulling my shirt up over my mouth and nose, and closed the door.

"C'mon sicko, let's get you to bed," I said through the protective layer of fabric and steered her shoulders as we walked up the stairs.

"I can do it myself. You're gonna be late." She swayed as we walked. Even through her shirt, her shoulders felt like red coals.

"I know you can," I said as I got her to her bed. She laid down and I propped her head up with a pillow. I pulled the blankets up over her as far as they would go and tucked her in, she was shaking like a chihuahua. "I'm gonna make you some tea. Chamomile with honey, okay?"

"Uh huh," she mumbled, probably half asleep already in her blanket cocoon.

I knew her house like I knew mine: where the tea was kept, how the dishes were arranged, how the honey would definitely be all the way in the back of the tallest cabinet just out of reach so I would have to precariously balance on a kitchen chair to get it. I knew the Aldersons didn't have a kettle so I just microwaved it—a travesty, I know—but I did what I could with what little I had. Grabbing Thea's "World's

Best Director" mug, which she bought herself to quote-unquote speak her dreams into existence, I poured in the freshly radiated water and tossed in the teabag. Nearly dying in the process, I grabbed the honey and stirred in a copious amount because I knew Thea well enough to know that if I didn't, she wouldn't drink it.

I looked for a small towel and got it a little damp, hoping to cool her forehead. I knew where she kept her monthly emergency heating pad, so I grabbed that as well. Precariously, I made my way back up the stairs and to her room and, to no surprise, she was already asleep. Oh well. I set the tea on her nightstand, the towel on her forehead, and the heating pad by her feet before taking a seat on the edge of her bed.

She looked like a porcelain doll, but in the way that porcelain dolls never look human. Too pale while also too red. Something just slightly off about the shape of the nose, the color of the eyes, the placement of the cheekbones. Something alien.

I blamed myself the instant I saw her. I don't know why, well no that's not entirely true, I did know why but I know it's a stupid reason: I didn't bring an umbrella on Wednesday. Why is that a reason to blame yourself for Thea getting sick, you may be asking, or you've already connected the dots like the genius you are, but to put things bluntly Thea's a bit incapable of taking care of herself. It rained on Wednesday, y'see, and Thea never ever not once has ever had an umbrella on her person when she needs one. I, however, normally do and, because I didn't have classes that required me to leave the singular multi-department D-wing, I'd give her my umbrella for the day with the promise of it being returned by rehearsal. Thanks to this lapse in my memory, Thea turned up to rehearsal drenched from head to toes, from skin to bones. Surely that was the cause, I thought and still think.

If only the routine was met and my umbrella had remained in my bag, if only I hadn't diverted from my version of normal. Dramatic, yes, but I was a theatre kid, remember?

～

I had lost track of time getting Thea prepped for a day of dripping in snot and sweat so I decided that first period wasn't all that important anyway and grabbed a coffee at some shitty drive thru that was nothing compared to the Roast. I ended up throwing the cup out when it was about halfway done as I could simply not ingest the horror that was my iced coffee turned milkshake by some buffoon of a barista. The scone I'd ordered to go with it had to be eaten shamefully and dry as I signed my tardy slip in the front office before getting to second period. The simple cramps excuse always stops further questions or any repercussions from the very male, very macho Vice Principal Gordon, I've learned that thanks to many a morning coffee run with T. If she were with me, maybe the iced garbage would have been bearable.

Classes went by painfully slow, which was a refreshing and much needed return to routine for the day, but the lunch bell eventually rang as it always did at 12:41pm and released us from our self-contained laminate-and-blue-plastic prison cells. We may be inferiors in the eyes of most teachers, but we were still due some basic rights like sunlight and sustenance. Not that I would partake in either, my feet taking me straight to the theatre.

"Hey Jane! Where's T? She wasn't there for the wonderful surprise of Wretched's class today," Valerie said through a mouthful of cold pizza. I once again was reminded why I felt just a twinge of sympathy for the horrible substitute that was Ms. Gretchen.

"She's sick." I plopped my bag into the seat of a desk and sat atop it, kicking my rubber-toed shoes back and forth, back, and forth. "We still on for the movie? I know it was kind of her idea."

"Oh shit, sorry Jane but I totally forgot that my mom needs me to babysit today. Some sort of work thing." Val rolled her eyes and groaned, throwing her head back onto Victor's shoulder.

He gave the top of her head one or two empathy pats and then chimed up, "I could always come and help, if you'd like? I need the practice anyway." We all chuckled at this. "I'm sure Eddie's still down though, if you're worried, Jane."

As my mother says, mostly to her clients but sometimes to my brothers and me, speak of the devil and he will appear. Before Valerie even had enough time to accumulate another mouthful of cold peperoni, pineapple, and jalapeno (gross, I know), Eddie flung the door open and walked in with the force of a hurricane. This force died down to the pathetic sprinklings of a single grey cloud, however, as he approached the group.

"Uh, Eddie, all good there, bud?" Victor was the one to break the silence.

With his usual flare somehow muted, Eddie wilted into an empty chair, his head in his hands and a rolled stack of papers clutched in one fist.

We waited, knowing he'd speak his mind without being provoked further.

"D! –She gave me a D!" We connected the dots and then she quickly became Ms. Saechao, his biology teacher, and the class he had to sit through before lunch.

On and on went the rant of how hard he'd studied, which was a lie, and how unfair it was, which was also a lie, until finally he sighed and said, "I've got to start getting my shit together."

I patted his back and suggested the tutoring sessions she held after school on Fridays. Why did I know about these? Well, I had a life before theatre and an interest in biology thanks to the weird genealogy of my family. Occasionally I would go and help some of the students who weren't detrimentally lost but simply had a couple of questions. That all stopped once rehearsals became a part of my day-to-day. With my life having been as busy as it was, I couldn't have been expected to keep everything together, to let nothing slip through the cracks.

"Yeah…yeah that's genius, Jane! If I go to tutoring, on a Friday of all days, she'll feel so bad for me that my grade will undoubtedly change out of pure pity!" Eddie beamed, his emotional state a constant pendulum that swung every which way.

Not exactly what I meant, but not in the mood to argue or discuss all the ways he was wrong, I replied with a nod and half-smile that implied both sympathy and hope. He bought it and rushed off to go tell Ms. Saechao he'd see her after school, going as quickly as he came.

"Looks like I'll be a party of one today," I chuckled before Valerie piped up.

"No, there's still one person who hasn't cancelled."

I felt the blood drain from my face. Why did we invite him anyway?

↝↝

"So yeah…everyone else bailed," I sighed, chewing on the straw of my iced coffee as I waited for Beckett to hang up his barista-boy apron and visor that I decided, on the flip of a coin, not to steal that day.

"Do you still want to go?" He glanced back at me with pleading dichromatic eyes. I could tell the answer was a yes for him as soon as his gaze met mine. People say the eyes are the mirror of the soul and if that's true he must have two.

It took me by surprise, really. He was so earnest, from iris to pupil with his answer that I couldn't help but laugh. I've always been one to laugh when things are too serious, too tense. Helps break things down for me, but also manages to get me into a fair amount of trouble. Remember Ms. Wretched? Yeah, I stopped pitying her pretty quickly after she didn't take too kindly to one of these laughing fits.

I thought for a moment before concluding that the worst that would happen was that it was a shit movie, which I had already expected it to be.

"Sure."

⌇⌇⌇

"What are you doing?" I couldn't help but chuckle as Beckett opened the back door to my car—my mom's old bright blue minivan, don't get too jealous. "I'm not a chauffeur, y'know?"

He quickly shut the door and laughed that awkward kind of laugh you make when you're not quite sure you get the joke. "Sorry, sorry. Front seat's just usually been reserved for Thea," he said as he got in and buckled up. As I adjusted my rear-view, I silently questioned if his lanky form even weighed enough to set off the seatbelt alarm.

I shook my head, a slight hmm, not quite a laugh but not quite a quip, buzzing through my lips as the engine started with a hum. That hum became the only noise to fill the air before Beckett spoke up.

"Thanks for driving."

"Not like I had a choice."

"Could've made me walk."

I laughed at the thought of Beckett running alongside my car as I drove to the theatre. I can't say it wasn't tempting to have him get out at that very moment, but I didn't. The hum returned as our laughter died down.

"Y'know, this is the first time we've actually hung out, just us."

"Really?" I hadn't thought about it before, but he was right. Even the day we met; Thea was there, just as she always was. He'd guessed my name just based on our coffee order, the fact that I "don't look like the creamer type" and Thea does, apparently, whatever that means. Every time I'd seen him since, she was there or the whole gang was. The only time I'd been alone with him was in that closet or at the counter, but even then, T was close behind. "I guess you're right. Weird."

As I pulled up to the theatre, I was grateful there were fewer people to make fun of my parking job; it's never been a strong suit of mine and the gang couldn't help but remind me. Beckett, however, didn't even mention it. For once, I found myself thankful for his presence.

He tried to pay for both our tickets, but I reminded him that I am both strong and independent. He tried to hold the door, but I walked through the one adjacent to it. I defied his chivalry at every turn, trying to kill it even. Chivalry is indeed dead, and I've always believed it should remain six feet under.

When it came to snacks, he relented and ordered first.

"Can I get a medium popcorn and a large cup half filled with vanilla soft served, half with cherry slushie?"

"A what?" I looked at him, aghast. The staff member seemed to have either dealt with his kind before or seen far stranger and simply fulfilled the order.

"I know it sounds weird, but you can't knock it 'til you try it," he grinned as if this monstrous concoction was a window into his soul and him sharing it with me was some sort of massive gesture.

I ordered the much more normal pack of peanut M&M's and a blue raspberry slushie. I can't quite explain what it is, but movie theatres require slushies to be ordered; a soda feels far too pedestrian. "I don't think I'd try it if you paid me."

"Don't be like that. You really should try it."

I did, and it was slightly less disgusting than I imagined but I'd never tell him that. His look of disappointment as I grimaced was far too earned.

We got into the screening room just before the movie began, but honestly, I wish we missed a bit of it. It was just as horrid as expected, unlike that odd slushie concoction, but enjoyable because we laughed through the whole thing. As he offered me popcorn, I could swear our hands touched just like in the movies but we both pulled away before we thought the other noticed. We dug a grave into that popcorn, not knowing who it was for.

As I drove him home, the rain picked up again did and ran down the windows, each droplet starting and stopping at their own pace.

"Y'know, I used to pretend the raindrops were racecars," Beckett said.

"Used to?" I arched a brow.

"Okay, okay, still do." His shoulders shook as he chuckled, but his face was turned away, gazing out at the rain. "I can't help it. They're so unpredictable sometimes. One seems to be moving forward when, bam, it just stops, or better yet the one that was lagging behind the whole time picks up speed to win. I dunno. I just think they're fun to watch."

"Well, I did and do the same thing. No need to explain it to me," I said, not sure why I said it. It was true but I knew how dumb it was. "I used to pretend the car ate the lines that divide the lanes."

"Used to?" Beckett mocked.

My lips curled to a slight smile. "Still do."

The movie was nothing special, neither was the day, but it was a fun break from the constant speeding pace that rehearsals brought to my life, nonetheless. His company was a good change, better than going to the movies alone, so we agreed to do it again. It would eventually become our thing, stupid movies, the way we got away from the chaos the gang brought and to our own bit of secluded peace with strange dessert amalgamations and often rainy drives afterward.

Pulling up to Beckett's house, which was nicer than I'd imagined it to be, he got out and waved from the door. The short walk from driveway to doorway left him soaked to the bone so I braved the weather enough to roll down the window to laugh at him. As he got inside and my window made its arduous way back up, I checked my phone to see a message from T.

"Thank you for taking care of me. Sorry to bail, hope you had fun on your day off anyway" it read.

I thought for a moment before typing my response.

"I did."

CHAPTER 9

Family Firsts

Since you've made it this far, I'm sure you've got a pretty good grasp of who I am but here's something that hasn't come up, at least not much: I'm not amazing at time management, but I hate people who are even worse. T's one of those people who lets time get away from her like each minute is a penny and she's a millionaire. She's able to make commitments and stick to them, but that's only ever applied to theatre and me.

Yesterday, it stopped applying to me. Something changed.

I sat there, latte in hand, at my favorite study spot on campus, directly across from a lovely little grove of trees where everyone hangs up hammocks and thus the best spot on campus to watch people fall out of hammocks and waited. And waited. And waited. The ringing went on until it inevitably chimed with her familiar "Future director Thea Alderson here, sorry I couldn't catch your call, I'm probably busy prepping for the Tonys! I'll ring you back asap, bye" voicemail prompt. I sighed, pondered for a moment, and tried again. Nothing.

This wasn't just an out-of-the-blue call, which would have made her inability to answer far easier to stomach. No, it was our weekly call time. Which she set up, mind you. There's a Google Calendar invite and everything, I even have it circled on my whiteboard calendar, which was my compromise with my mother. She said paper calendars were out of date, I said I'll never check my phone calendar so whiteboard it was. But my choice of organization is far from the point. The point is that Thea diverted from our regularly scheduled programming.

I wondered if this is how my brothers, my mother, my father, even my cat felt when my focuses shifted: rejected. But this wondering didn't last long because I knew that they did, in fact, feel the same. Selfishly, like the teenage kid I was, I didn't notice until I was basically hit over the head, Des of all people having been the one to wield the bat.

～

There was a time in my life when my family was the center of my attention. Like everyone, this began to die down once I reached my teenage years, but I'd say I was a late bloomer in this regard. Well, more than just this regard but I see no reason to get into all of that. What I really mean is that I had no friends other than Thea for quite some time and to make up for this lack of social interaction I spent my time with those who couldn't avoid spending time with me.

I was the kid who jumped at the chance to accompany my dad to his office's "bring your kid to work" day. Desmond and Norman never felt the need; They actually had friends and lives even at such a tender age. My father was not disappointed by their dismissal and my eagerness, though, as I'd always thought myself to be his secret favorite. Daddy's girl stereotype and all that, y'know? Thick as thieves, we were and a good number of my favorite memories occurred in his office, encapsulated by those soft orange walls.

Or at least I thought so.

His office was the most interesting in the building. How could it not be? He worked with animals and all the other psychologists worked with people, an ever less interesting medium if I have anything to say about it.

The posters were always my favorite. You'd think they'd be fun and playful, perhaps a kitten hanging from a branch with some sort of hang in there pun above its head in Comic Sans, but no. My father had a more unique taste, more macabre. It explains his interest in my mother, I used to think to myself when staring at the posters.

The skinless anatomical models and skeletal figures, picture-perfect and capturing every detail, would be enough to give normal children nightmares but for all my boring qualities I am anything but normal. Average, yes, but not normal. Not normal enough to look away at the grotesque diagrams but instead just abnormal enough to find bits of intrigue in each. For a while these posters made me think I may be a biologist but that was before I acquired my distaste for dissection. I found that it's quite different when you're the one doing the slicing.

During these days, my dad would have me sit in the hallway during his sessions, but they never took long because he's good at what he does. Unlike humans, once the answer to the problem is found, more problems do not arise. That's just the end of the session. The trauma tends to be not so deep-seated. I'd just sit and trace lines in the hexagonal patterned carpet and wait until whatever creature he was assessing, and their owner, found whatever closure they sought.

When there were no patients, though, was when I was allowed to gawk at the posters and he told me all about every muscle, every bone, every ligament and vein and nerve he knew on every single one of them. It didn't matter how many times he'd gone over them; I'd always want to hear the alien-sounding medical terminology again.

"What about that one? What's that one called?" I'd asked, jumping on my tiptoes to try and reach up and touch the smallest, most insignificant looking bone I could.

"That's one of the caudal vertebrae," he'd chuckle and lift me onto his shoulders so I could get a better look.

"It's so small!" My eyes would squint to near shut to see it: the tip of a cat's tail.

"Small, yes, but that's because each individual joint connects. It's a small part of a bigger picture." He'd set me down and ruffle my hair.

As a child, I thought of these chats as a coded language, something only he and I could ever share. Now, I realize I was likely right.

<div style="text-align:center">~~~</div>

While my brothers never cared to accompany me on these journeys to our dad's workplace, they found other ways to spend time with me, either together as a singular unit of annoyance or separately, a state where they were both more enjoyable to be around.

I'd never tell either of them, but I did have a favorite. The favorite was a rotation, whichever one was being less of a nuisance, which commonly happened to be Norman. Don't get me wrong, when Desmond was being a tolerable human being, he was a delight to be around. Norman and I just happened to mesh better most of the time. He and I happened to be more awkward, quieter, less likely to be the ones to make a decision. We were the wallflowers; Desmond was the one tearing the wall apart. He was what I liked to refer to as the wrecking ball of the family.

With Des and Nor, it never was a competition for who had more energy like it tends to be between boys. They both had plenty of energy, too much of it, some including myself may say, but their outlets were different. Norman was always trying to learn, he was reading at an absurd pace, one that my parents couldn't keep up with in regard to supplying more material for him to devour.

It got so bad he eventually started reading the back of cereal boxes aloud every morning during breakfast, trying to see how much he could recite in a single breath. It drove me crazy and I'm sure the others weren't the biggest fans. My father never let us silence him, though, because it was important to his intellectual and social growth to determine when an appropriate time was to babble on, or something like that. But he didn't get quiet for years. I got pretty good at tuning him out, too, so I'm not quite sure what his reasoning was.

Desmond, on the other hand, preferred silent expression. You'd think this would make him more tolerable, but no, it was the opposite most of the time. He was the schemer, the one who knew exactly what to say to get under your skin or derail a conversation entirely. A panther in wait, stalking his prey, he'd pounce into a conversation seeking nothing but to destroy it. It was as if he held his breath to speak, waiting for that perfect moment to exhale when his lungs were just dying for it.

It took time, adjusting to their existence, their patterns, and their ticks, but eventually, I managed. I seemed to manage better than our parents, who often are at a loss with the twins. I was the bridge between this gap, understanding them before their own parents did. There were times, of course, when I couldn't quite get them either.

〜

It was early, earlier than we normally liked to get up on the weekends when our parents decided we needed to get out for the day as a family. It wasn't something we did extremely often due to both my parents having somehow thriving careers. They only got a concurrent day off once in a blue moon so that one Saturday morning they'd decided to take advantage of it. The weather wasn't particularly nice, a bit on the cloudy side, and the drive was longer than three children could bear without asking the dreaded "are we there yet" but in spite of it all, my parents decided upon a beach day.

As rare as it was for us to have a family day, it was even rarer for us to go anywhere nearer to the coast than our hometown of Gaithersburg. My mother was prone to sunburns, as were the twins, and my father pretended he knew how to swim. He didn't, and we all knew it. We just let him pretend he was cramping, or busy, or enjoying the sun, or whatever excuse he tried to use. The only reason to really go to the beach was me.

I liked the water and the sand, sure, but those weren't what drew me to the beach. I liked to see all the bits and pieces people left behind or those that were lost and got washed ashore. Sometimes it was a stray shoe, a towel, even a toy, but it was most commonly, unsurprisingly and yet still disappointingly, trash. Still, I had hopes of finding treasure at the beach one day, finding the map to a pirate's lost hoard that somehow ended up buried in the sands of Maryland of all places. Foolish, I know, but the dreams of children often are.

So we went to the beach, where I would spend all day combing the sand for trinkets and trash and my brothers were likely to remain under an umbrella and by our mother's side all day and my father would step out to wade ankle-deep in the ocean's tide but never a drop more. That was how I expected the day to go, at least, but it didn't.

On my end all went just according to plan, I'm boring like that and tend to stick to my patterns, though there was an unaccounted-for bit of company.

Desmond.

We were young and while our trek together felt perilous, I doubt we ever left our parents' sight. Even so, I felt as though I needed to take charge, make sure nothing occurred that would injure either of us, or, worse, land us in trouble. The silence that was his personality, at least what I surmised it to be, was astounding and I found myself filling Norman's babbling shoes.

"You've gotta keep an eye out, okay? I don't wanna miss anything cool because you're here distracting me."

He nodded and I was sure he wasn't listening. I could feel my cheeks burning red with frustration. I later learned it was the UV rays burning my skin but the emotion behind it remained.

"I'm serious, you know. There's bound to be something really awesome and you're not gonna be the one to screw it up." I meant to say it teasingly, but I'm sure it came off a lot harsher than intended thanks to the face he made in response. No sound though. It sure was hard to get a rise out of that kid. Luckily for me as an older sister, as that is my primary job, this inability faded with age.

We spent what felt like hours combing through the sand, find shells and wrappers and broken bits of glass that'd been smoothed down to gems, but nothing that I was looking for. Nothing that screamed treasure. Then I saw a glint of light bounce off a dune ahead of me. I ran for it. I plopped down to my knees and scooped away the sand, dug until there was sand beneath my fingernails and embedded in the skin of my kneecaps, but it was for naught. The inside-out empty bag of Lays that laid before me was all my digging and searching got. And then I turned, and Desmond was not behind me. Instead, he was making a mad dash for the water like it called to him.

"Des!" I yelled after him, leaving behind my treasured trash. He dove in. By the time I made it to the water's edge, he was in and out. Whatever goal he'd had, he accomplished it before even my parents took notice. I grabbed his soaking wet shoulders and shook him. "Des what in the world?! What were you thinking?!" I didn't even have the time to grimace at how much like an adult I sounded yelling at him like that. I felt a cold wet disk in the palm of my hand as soon as he took mine in his.

"I was finding treasure," he said, and I swear that was the first time I saw him smile. Like really smile.

The coin, which was the closest thing to a gold doubloon I'd ever seen, was nothing special in the end. A dollar in Hong Kong or something like that, an odd-looking chunk of silver metal with squiggly edges.

But to me, and though I never asked him I assumed that to Desmond, it was something to be treasured.

～

"You sure are spending a lot of time with those theatre nerds," Des chimed in, his mouth full of cereal and milk dripping from the corners of his lips as he spoke.

Norman would have commented, but his habit of reading the backs of cereal boxes stuck with him throughout the years. Luckily, he learned how to stop doing it aloud. Each chemical compound was something they could ask him about during the next Science Olympiad or whatever, I had a hard time keeping up with him when he started rambling about his smart people competitions.

Normally, I would've gotten to avoid Desmond's judgmental quips but alas he was off from swim for once that Saturday morning. The pool got overchlorinated and likely would've left all the kids with chemical burns. Norman offered to readjust the water's pH by adding bases to balance out the levels of hydrochloric and hypochlorous acid, but the swim coach and the science teacher wanted him to stay away from chemicals on school grounds on account of the incident.

Don't worry, both of their eyebrows have grown back. Kind of. But none of this is the point. The point is that Desmond was busying himself during this newfound free time by bothering me about what I did with mine.

"Yeah, what of it?" Rather than cereal, I was drinking a cup of coffee and slicing through a stack of waffles. The kind you stick in a toaster, nothing fancy. Saturdays were busy for the 'rents what with all of dad's patients and all of mom's clients having time during the weekends, so we usually fended for ourselves when it came to breakfast and lunch. This was made up for by the promise of takeout for dinner, so we didn't mind.

"I'll be home late!" Dad would yell as he struggled to get his left shoe on—always the left for some reason—and himself out the door. I enjoyed this moment of chaos, as it allowed me to see which animal print sock he'd be wearing. That day it was meerkats.

"What do you mean the Masons want to see the Beall-Dawson House? Just yesterday they were asking for a spot as close as they could manage to the Maryland Mine!" Mom would rush down the stairs in full Morticia Adams garb. Her clients didn't want to see pastels or lip gloss, they wanted the full haunted home buying experience, outfit of their agent, and all. She'd even do her hair with a bit of Elvira flair just for good luck on closing days.

We knew better than to bother her when she was mid-call with flip-flopping buyers, so we'd let her storm off and just hope she realized that shirt was a button off or her shoes were mismatched on the way to the listing. She always did.

"Well, it's just that you used to spend more time around the house or at Thea's is all." Norman glanced up from his cereal box.

"What I think he means is that it's nice to see you making friends for once," Desmond chirped.

"That's not what I meant!"

"It totally is."

"Is not!"

Their bickering went back and forth for a few moments as I pondered what Des said. I suppose I was making friends, but I'd had friends before. Just none as close as T and I, but I think that's almost a good thing. Relationships like that are either once in a lifetime or toxic.

Eddie was quickly reaching the summit some may call "best-friendship" and Victor and Valerie weren't far behind, though they were better suited together than interacting outside of their bubble of a world. Even Beckett was someone I'd call a friend, though I'd never tell him that. I guess Des was right, I was making friends. But it's not like I needed them. I'd had T, after all. What more could I have needed?

I pushed my chair out and stood up. "While you two are busy, I've gotta get going. Rehearsals start soon."

Norman stood up as well. "Wait, can you give me a ride? Janice and Theo want to study flashcards at Page Turners."

I hesitated, debating telling him no just because I'm an older sister and that's what we're supposed to do, but shrugged. It's not like the eclectic little bookshop, owned by you guessed it the Turners, was out of the way.

~~

"He misses you, y'know?" Norman slung his bookbag over his shoulder and, before I could get another word out of him, the door to Page Turners was swinging shut.

What was he talking about? Desmond? Missing me? That was hysterical to me. He and I were close, sure, but he'd grown up and so had I. We weren't treasure hunters anymore; we hadn't been for a long time. There was nothing to miss, I thought as I pulled into my usual parking space behind the theatre.

Thea and the others swarmed the car, not even giving me a moment to breathe before whisking me off to whatever the hell kind of world that classroom became when we entered. Rehearsal was fine, nothing out of the ordinary. Mitchell was late and brought donuts as his usual apology.

On my way out, I texted Nor if he'd need a ride. No response. Figured he was busy with his flashcards, so I drove home. Des wasn't there when I walked in so I figured he must have found something to do with his day off. With time to myself, which was a rare commodity, I decided I'd do what any high schooler would do: take a nap.

As unlikely as it was for everyone to be home at once, it felt even more unlikely to be home alone. Usually, a brother was there to pester me, or a mom was there to ask in a thinly veiled way if I were gay which would be fine except I'm not and never was, or a dad to give advice where none was asked for. I can't say I was truly home alone, though, as there would always be Mr. Socks.

An aptly named little beast, our cat Mr. Socks was all black except for his paws, three of which were white, and one was orange. Don't ask me where the orange one came from, none of us are really sure. We just assumed he was some sort of calico mix and left it be. If the sock had changed colors on occasion, well maybe we'd be more likely to raise questions.

But nevertheless, I wasn't alone because he was there, staring at me judgmentally from the top of my "trophy shelf." We all had one, us kids, but I was the only one who never used mine. Desmond had his swimming medals and Norman had his academic awards, but all I had was the barren wooden shelf that could have only ever housed a recreational soccer participation trophy. I had enough pride, however, to refrain from doing so and that worthless trophy surely ended up in some memory box stored away in the attic or garage or somewhere hopefully no one will ever find it and remind me that my shelf is a wasteland.

It's not like I really cared, though. I didn't do anything award-worthy so why would I have any? It's not like I won spelling bees or track meets, it's not like I even participated in anything like that. It's not like I participated. That was, at least, until Thea roped me into doing something with my life, but that's not what we're discussing at the moment.

We're not discussing the number of times during a 'take your kid to work' day a pet patient and their owner would leave my father's office and ask who I was and if I was lost. We're not discussing how, when I told them I was there with my dad, they'd ask who my dad was. Or how when I told them they were just talking to him, they'd more often then not say they didn't realize Dr. Carter had a daughter. Not kids, just a daughter. We're not discussing how I didn't blame them, or him for that matter, and how I'd allowed myself to expect that response and we're certainly not discussing how I wouldn't have mentioned me to any of his patients either. What was there to mention? Desmond was talented, Norman was brilliant, and I was…there. Just there.

Instead, we're discussing how my cat meowed and mewed from that empty shelf, staring down at me as if he knew nothing would ever go on it.

"What?" I muttered through my pillow up at him. The good thing about having an empty trophy shelf is that Mr. Socks had no trophies to knock down onto me while I laid there. My brothers, judging from their late-night one-sided arguments, did suffer from this. He didn't respond, obviously, but instead leapt down onto my back with a thud.

He batted my face as my eyes drifted shut. Nowadays I find myself wishing I'd played with him more, petted him more.

<p style="text-align:center">~~~</p>

"Rehearsals again? You said you'd come to my meet," Desmond spoke so quickly he nearly choked on the oatmeal he'd been eating.

"It's not like you really want me there," I said as if I knew, spinning my keyring around a finger. "Just text me when you need a ride, okay? And at least tell me if the team goes out for pizza or something afterwards this time. I don't want to wait at the pool for an hour worrying again."

I didn't give him the chance to respond. I probably should've, but it took me until later in life to realize that even brothers have feelings. They'll never tell you them, at least not outright, but they're there. Somewhere buried deep in machismo and Cheeto dust, yes, but they're there.

Rehearsals went the same, though I could feel the date of opening night approaching, stalking up on me. It was a feeling like no other. This wasn't just a test or an assignment, this was something I actually found myself caring about. I was nervous like I'd never been nervous before but who could I say that to? My father, who would psychoanalyze it? My brothers, who would laugh? My mother who…god knows what she'd do but I can guarantee that, back then, anything she would've said would've made it worse. That's just how mothers were to daughters in high school. I'd eventually grow out of this feeling, but that day was not the day.

As I got in my car and contemplated my nerves, I felt a buzzing in my back pocket.

"Can you pick me up?" It was a text from Desmond, followed soon after by, "Still at the pool."

"Sure."

My brother stood outside the swim complex with a medal around his neck and a towel around his shoulders. He was still soaking wet, but my car had seen worse, so I had relented a while back to let him hop in before drying off. "Looks like things went well."

"Yeah," he mumbled. I hated when he mumbled. It made him hard to understand and it meant something was wrong, meaning I'd have to ask what it was. It's not like he'd return the favor, neither of the twins really would, but for some reason, I always feel like it's my job to ask: my responsibility to do so. Why I feel this way, I couldn't say. Perhaps it's because our parents were often busy, perhaps it's because boys are always so emotionally constipated. Whatever the reason, I knew I had to ask.

"What's wrong?"

I knew better than to expect an answer, at least a clear one. I drove in silence for some time, eventually turning onto the highway. A still silence clung to the air as the water droplets clung to my brother's hair. He didn't move and neither did they, floating there as if frozen. As if life had hit the pause button for even just a moment. I couldn't help but feel a small sense of relief, a bit of catharsis at this rest in the concerto that is life as we know it.

This silence, though welcomed at first, held weight and that weight built, it grew, it bred, and soon was all that populated the air between the windshields. They say silence is deafening but it's not. It's just thick and heavy and caustic. Breathing in this toxic silence, I couldn't focus on the road or on the headlights shining behind me or the rain cascading down. I pulled off on the first exit I saw, an exit we usually never took. It was the exit that led to the unfinished overpass.

There were legends and tales about this overpass. Some girl jumped off it and haunts it, you'll get abducted by aliens if you sit there on a full moon, all the hokey urban storytelling that occurs almost anywhere. Nobody believed the stories, of course, but even so, the place was elevated not only by concrete pillars but by word of mouth. The more you spoke of it, the more it infected your mind. The overpass was what I liked to call an urban virus.

And yet it was, in that moment, a cure.

"What are you doing?" Desmond's voice pierced the air and spread out in soundwaves, disturbing the surface of thick pools of quiet.

"I don't know."

"Where are we going?"

"I said I don't know."

I pulled up to the top of the overpass, right up to the dead-end signs to the point that the bumper just barely scraped the rusty metal and took a few flecks of chipped paint away as a trophy. My first. The scraping wasn't intentional, at least I think it wasn't. I was too busy doing anything to keep the silence away to be able to give a definitive answer nowadays.

Stepping out into the rain, I heard every plummet of every drop. Every plink against each chain of the chain-link fence keeping us from falling from the abandoned overpass. I listened to the rushing of every micro-stream created in each crack in the asphalt, of the waterfall created off the edge of the overpass, of the blood flowing into my heart, out of my heart, into my heart. I was listening so intently that I almost missed the opening and slamming of the car door, the sloshing footsteps of bare feet on wet concrete, the calling of my name through the rain.

"Jane, what are we doing here?"

I didn't need to look at Des to paint his picture in that moment. The rain clung to his chlorine-soaked hair and his rain-soaked clothes clung to his skin like algae to wet stone. His teeth chattered as he spoke and who could blame him? It was by no means lovely weather and the kid was in running shorts and a t-shirt, the same outfit he wore before and after every meet. It was his routine, his regimen, his ritual.

Again, I didn't need to look at him to know what he looked like or how he shivered or how his eyes held both an incredulous and apologetic look. I was as if he should be the one apologizing when I was the one who stopped without warning on the overpass. When I was the one to leave the car. When I was the one to miss the meet which I didn't bother to realize actually meant something to him.

"I'm sorry, Des."

The silence that followed reverberated off every raindrop, deafening. It kept bouncing from surface to surface, droplet to asphalt to chain in the fence, as we stood there, and it kept doing so as we entered the car and threatened to ruin the pleather interior with our presence.

It bounced from car door to window to seat to key and eventually, when it reached that final destination, I put the silence in the ignition and broke it with the hum of the engine. Desmond spoke up as I did, his voice almost hidden by the thrum of shitty station wagon. I heard him; whether he wanted me to or not remains up in the air to this day, but I believe he knows I did. If I hadn't heard him, if he hadn't intended for me to hear him, I'm not sure our relationship would be the same.

He said, "I know."

I wasn't sure he meant it, at least, I wasn't until I watched as, from the pocket of those running shorts, he pulled out a silver coin with squiggly edges and flipped it once.

CHAPTER 10

Opening Up

With our scheduled calls all but out the window, Thea and I had been, well, distant to say the least. Normally she would call first, but instead I'd been given the role of initiator. Normally we could have chat for hours on end, but recent calls had been twenty minutes max, if that. That week, our call was twenty seconds.

"Hey," I smiled into the phone, just happy she picked up.

"Hey! Can I call you back, J? I'm out with friends."

I was still smiling because at least I got to hear her voice. "Sure. No problem. Talk later?"

All I heard in response was the familiar beep of an ended call. No talk to you later, no miss you, no nothing. And I get it, I really do. She was with friends; she didn't have the time for me. That would have been fine and all if the day wasn't already a mess. But you don't need to hear about all that, no, you hear enough of that. It really wouldn't have been a big deal if she had actually called back.

Instead, I'm in bed, on a Saturday night, feeling far from alright. I can't help but hope my phone lights up with her name and face on my screen, but I know it won't.

Even my roommate, usually ambivalent towards my unending suffering, asked if I was alright. That's how you know I'm really in the shit. Alas, on days like these there's only one thing that can pick me up and, unfortunately, there's not a Roast in sight.

A Rainy Jane is just the thing for a rainy day.

Everyone has them, days where it feels like everything is falling apart and the world hates you, but, for me, these days seemed far more abundant, especially in high school. I'm sure every high school kid feels this way and I'm sure half of them are full of it, but I can assure you I was not. When things fell apart for me, they did so like dominoes, knocking one after the other down in an endless train of disaster.

But let's be realistic. What high school kid can even say they experienced an actual disaster? Very few, because melodrama and angst are two of the pubescent hormones, we, more often than not, tend to overlook. Especially in the drama club.

I can't even say I truly experienced any sort of disaster at that age, or any age really. Real disasters are reserved for people with real problems and my problems, I'm starting to think, were never as bad as they could be. Someone always has it worse, right? That's what everyone always says.

Rather than leave you in suspense about my days of unrelenting suffering, I'll walk you through one, a prime example. Y'see, it all started on a Monday, as all bad days do.

"Hey, J, wait up!" I heard a familiar voice ring out behind me as I trudged my way to third period. Thea ran up beside me and, in her rush to catch me, she must've forgotten to pump the breaks and her foot collided with the back of my heel, sending me flying forward.

So, forward I flew. Right into a just-opened locker door. The sound that was made when my face hit the thin metal door was something to behold, something for which the music teacher surely would have had some strange musical terminology. Our locker doors, to match our school colors, were blue. That day, the locker was red.

Luckily, I didn't make some girlish shriek or cry of pain. I like to think I took a locker door to the face with grace, but I'm sure anyone who saw the event would say otherwise. Thea was the one who let out a shriek, as she knelt by me and pulled out a pack of tissues.

"Y-you're bleeding," she said hurriedly, looking away from my grotesque visage.

She was, in fact, right I realized as I glanced down at my hands, which had instinctively clutched my face the moment it had disconnected from the aforementioned locker door. My palms were red and, when I looked up in a haze, there was a blur of red on the floor and the door. I grabbed hold of the tissue in her outstretched hand, putting it to my nose and feeling it soak through in a near-instant.

Blood never bothered me like it did T.

The opener of the locker door was stunned, though I couldn't see it. I gathered this based on their silence and the sound of their footsteps as they walked backward, away from the scene.

"Jane, Jane are you okay? How many fingers am I holding up? What's seven times three? What—?" Thea rambled on, panicked before I cut her off in a half groan.

"T, T, it's okay. I'm fine. You're holding up three fingers, that'd be twenty-one, calm down." I felt blood trickle into my mouth as I spoke. It tasted of iron and salt; I assume because it was probably mixed with snot. Gross, I know, but I suppose it was at least my own. Could have been worse.

Thea's doe eyes met mine, both of ours welling with tears, mine because I smacked my face real hard and hers because she caused it. "We should get you to the school nurse," she said, only half panicking this time. An improvement.

"Yeah? What are they going to do? Give me a soaked, frozen paper towel? Honestly T, I'll be fine. Bleeding just needs to stop is all." I tried to space my words out a little more to prevent the blood from continually seeping onto my tongue.

"Well, let's at least get out of the hallway," she semi-huffed as she dragged me to my feet. I didn't need to move the tissue to see where she was taking me, it had become second nature for my feet to walk the path towards classroom 231, otherwise known as every outcast's sanctuary, the theatre classroom.

Should we have gone to the school nurse? Maybe. Should we have gone to our actual class? Yes. But we were high school kids looking for someplace that resembled safety and privacy. That was anything but any other classroom. At least in theatre, we felt some semblance of security.

I didn't need to move the tissue out of my face to recognize the chatter of voices in the room, either. Should Eddie, Val, and Vic have been in their actual classes? Yeah, probably.

Did Mr. Mitchell care that we used his classroom as an escape from any other classroom? Honestly, I don't know. We probably should have asked him, but we were high school students which meant we were selfish, and this selfishness meant we did not see the side of anyone but ourselves as important or existent, for that matter.

"Hey, look who it is, our other half has arri—shit, Jane, you okay? What happened?" Valerie immediately jumped off the desktop she'd been sitting on and rushed to my aid.

"Ran into a locker, no biggie." I tossed the tissue and motioned to Thea for another one. She obliged.

Eddie and Victor laughed. I couldn't even blame them. After all, it was pretty funny. Thea and Valerie, however, shot them each a glare to shut them up. I appreciated the gesture.

That's when I heard Mitchell's tsking from behind. He stood, arms folded like a disapproving father, in the doorframe of his office. "Well, that's certainly a shame." We all looked at him in disbelief. His lack of concern should have been expected, we knew how he was, but even so. He was a teacher. I suppose he wasn't paid enough to care. "Our Juliet, our shining beauty, stuck with a broken nose so close to opening night. Should I phone an understudy?" he asked ruthlessly.

"It's not broken," Thea said defensively as if it were her nose on the line and not mine.

It was.

Now, you might be thinking this was a shame, sure, and that it was certainly the kind of disaster I was speaking of, yeah? You'd be wrong. It was the first drop of a flood.

~

"I told you, T, it's not a big deal. Stop apologizing already," I said to the voice of the void, the Thea Alderson on speakerphone, that flitted around my bathroom as I looked over my freshly unbandaged and newly sculpted nose in the mirror. I never thought I'd be the type to get even the slightest hint of a nose job. Those are typically set aside for girls whose daddies have money. My father, a pet psychologist, did not. The words *pet psychologist* should have tipped you off to that.

He did, however, have an extremely eccentric clientele, which, again, the words *pet psychologist* should have made obvious. One of whom happened to be a plastic surgeon of the stars. I'm sure anyone could connect the dots. A favor was called in and, bam, my nose was not only fixed but, in my eyes, transformed.

I would have settled for a Band-Aid and an ice pack but, no, nothing is too good for my father's daughter.

"I'm sorry, I won't stop apologizing because it makes me feel like I didn't totally disfigure my best friend!" the phone shouted out, the words, the segments, the phonemes bouncing off my walls in small echoes.

"T, it's been a week. Stop apologizing. Friday's opening night. You need to get your head in the game. You don't want this to be a disaster, do you?" I plopped down onto the counter.

A long pause. "No."

"Okay then. Get it together. Opening night is Friday. Friday! That's only four days away, T. Focus on what's happening in four days rather than on what happened seven days ago. The world kept spinning, nothing stopped."

"Okay, okay, I get it." Another pause. "Roast?"

"Always."

Less than five minutes later I found myself in the driver's seat, waiting in front of her house. She, like always, took her sweet time.

She gasped at the sight of me. "J! Look at you! You look like a whole new woman."

I rolled my eyes. "Same me. Nothing new about it."

Thea couldn't help but concede to my point when she turned the music up and I turned it right back down. "Same you."

~

The week was a blur, the kind left-handed people get on the side of their hand after turning in a long, handwritten essay. I suppose what I mean to say is that the week was a smudge. Insignificant. Easily wiped away. Rehearsal followed by dinner followed by sleep followed by breakfast followed by school followed by rehearsal. That was my week and, quite frankly, my high school career.

But then came Thursday night, where all was still until it wasn't.

As I closed my eyes for what was bound to be a night without sleep, my phone buzzed.

J from T

Yes?

Come get me from T

. . .

Please. from T

She didn't need to type another word.

Within seconds, I was in my car and headed to hers. It was a late night. I hadn't started to try to sleep until around two in the morning, so I had to slip out of the house silently. Parents would've freaked if they had known, but they didn't. It wasn't like I was doing anything crazy, anyway. I was going to Thea's.

As I pulled up, she was already waiting outside. That was warning sign one. Warning sign two was her attire. Thea's the kind of girl who likes to dress up to go anywhere. Her blanket-wrapped, pajama-bottoms-wearing-self did not seem even slightly prepared to go anywhere.

That's why I took us nowhere.

We sat in front of her house, the roar of the heater being the only sound for some time before she finally spoke up.

"What if I'm not good enough?"

I couldn't help but laugh. "What?"

She glared at me the kind of glare that stops a laugh in your throat. "I'm being serious."

"Good enough for what, T?" I asked after taking a moment to compose myself.

"Good enough for this," she motioned sporadically, "For theatre. For directing. For—" she stopped herself.

Silence consumed us. The fog of early morning clung to my headlights in a loose dew, creating a kaleidoscope effect of shadow and obscured light.

"T, you're plenty good enough to me."

On came the tears. Perhaps that was what she needed to hear, perhaps not. I'm not sure to this day. All I know is that she needed to cry, and I made her do it. As her tears streamed down her cheeks, I sat in awe of what seemed to be such a cathartic moment for her.

I know, actors and catharsis, we're obsessed with it, right? Wrong, at least in my case. I was in awe, but mostly I was bewildered. How could someone feel something so strongly? How could someone's soul be rocked by experience?

I didn't get it. Perhaps because I never felt anything that strongly or perhaps because I never feel anything strongly. I like to think I sort of just float through life but at this moment I was grounded in the fact that I didn't feel anything significant. I was just stating a fact, something I believed in wholeheartedly when I said Thea was plenty good enough. It wasn't meant to be a compliment, or something said just to flatter her, it was just the truth as I believed it.

~~

After a long and arduous week, of which almost nothing can I remember, it was time to finally show off the fruits of our semester-long labor. Our production of *Romeo and Juliet* would go off without a hitch, we all thought, especially given how much effort we put into it.

We were wrong and it was all my fault.

Now, that sounds like an over-exaggeration, doesn't it? Well, in all honesty, it probably is one. It's not like I set fire to the set or committed a felony, no, it's not that at all. What I did do, though, is commit a cardinal sin of theatre.

"Alright everybody, places people! The show's on in five, everyone better be ready by then!" Thea called out from over her shoulder as she laced up my corset in the girls' dressing room. In the corner of my eye, I could see the silent ticking of the seconds hand on the clock as it counted down to what would be my first time on a stage with a real audience. Sure, we'd had rehearsals but that was different.

This would be actual people here to see a performance. Pressure was on and tension was high. The air was so thick you could take a chunk out of it with a spoon, no knife needed.

"Calm down, T, everyone's either ready or almost ready. No need to stress," Valerie, of all people, said as Victor nodded in agreement. Now I suppose you could say that her job was done so of course she'd be calm, but Valerie was almost never calm. That was just her personality, one half of a powder keg waiting to blow. She was the one to try to talk Thea off her metaphorical cliff.

And let me tell you, telling a girl who's freaking out to calm down…not the wisest idea.

"Calm down? Calm down?!" Thea exclaimed, tightening the corset to an extreme that had me instinctively flailing. "I am calm!"

"T, T, I think you're killing her," Victor chimed in, gingerly pointing a finger in my direction. Only at his mentioning of my inability to breathe did Thea take note and act accordingly.

"Sorry J, –didn't mean to take that out on you," she mumbled, loosening the strings, and thus allowing air to rush back into my deprived lungs.

"It's fine, just maybe chill out a little?" I coughed, shooing her to the side as I was able to finish tightening the top bit of the corset.

"Where's Eddie?" I asked once I was finished, a bit concerned that my co-lead was nowhere to be found.

"Oh, don't worry," Victor said.

"He's probably in a closet somewhere getting in character," Valerie finished his statement before he could manage.

"Ironic, huh?" Thea giggled, making the obvious joke.

We all laughed, continuing the make small talk with the few minutes we had before showtime. Eddie eventually made himself known, making as grand an entrance as you can imagine. We all chatted away the final moments until we were stood behind a stage, silent for what felt like years but was only truly seconds.

If only we knew all our work would be wasted on my failure.

Curtain call went fine. Honestly, a lot of the show went off without a hitch. It was, for the most part, fantastic. Especially when the fact that it was a high school performance is considered, that makes it all the more impressive. It was this fact, however, that was also detrimental.

The thing about high school performances is, well, they're put on by high schoolers. High schoolers, as many people can surmise, are some of the worst creatures on the planet. They're emotionally driven to a fault, meaning if one little thing happens that throws them off, they're sure to raise hell. And that's what happened here.

I wouldn't say I've ever been a true high schooler in that I've never been so emotionally driven that it hurts me in the long run, but that night was anything but ordinary Jane Carter behavior.

Everything was going fine. Lines were flowing from my lips with the same precision and poise they had held during rehearsals. It seemed like this would be the perfect show, but no, it wasn't. It wasn't and it was all because of me.

"Oh Romeo, Romeo, wherefore art thou Rome—oh."

My gaze drifted between members of the audience as I delivered this famous line. I was trying to make every audience member feel as though they were part of the show. Mr. Mitchell had given me this tip during one of our rehearsals. It wasn't anything major, nothing hard to do, just make brief eye contact with a person and, bam, they're hooked on you and the show. Great advice, honestly. Something really simple to do while you're probably already going to be scanning the audience or looking off in that direction.

It would've worked perfectly if my gaze hadn't drifted to him.

There he was, sat in the front row as if a seat had been reserved. Beckett. The last person I wanted to see at that moment of vulnerability. I'd been vulnerable with him before, sure, but the type of vulnerability you feel on the stage is so much different from the type you feel in a closet. And, at that moment, I wanted to feel nothing like how I did.

So, I stopped.

I stopped feeling, stopped doing, stopped being, and, most importantly, I stopped acting. This pause in being wasn't long, perhaps a few seconds in totality, but it was enough that I saw the way Mitchell looked at me, the way Eddie looked at me, the way Thea looked at me. They were all stunned, sure, and maybe a little concerned, sure, but I think, most importantly, they were disappointed.

I froze. I stood there, up on that stage, in corset and all, and I froze. After months of rehearsals, I froze. After all their faith was placed in me, I froze.

Even so, the show must go on and go on it did. I snapped out of it and delivered my next line and the one after that, everything continued forward though there was this undertone of dread to my whole performance I'm sure as I knew Mitchell and Thea were waiting backstage to chew me out. Eddie was onstage and ready to chew me out. The only face in the audience that didn't hold some semblance of disappointment was his.

At the end of it all, we received a standing ovation, surely no part due to me. When I gave my bow, I could sense the audience's trepidation when it came to clapping for me. I could sense that I had let them down, had failed to reach their expectations.

As I headed off stage and towards our classroom for the post-show meeting, I felt every muscle in my body tense, ready for the storm that was coming my way.

"And Jane," Mitchell spoke up, having started giving his little spiel without me and Eddie since we were the last to leave the stage after our bows.

I cleared my throat, steeling my nerve.

"Good effort."

Those two words shattered my world. I felt the hot lava of tears running down my cheeks before my brain had time to process each phoneme. Good effort? He saw, he knew. What worse could he have said in that moment?

The apathy in his voice cut sharper than any knife, the disappointment in his eyes hit harder than a bus. My face burned with every syllable he spoke, and I stopped even being able to hear them, I could only recognize his speech by the movement of his lips and the faint buzzing that registered in my mind. Surely, he continued to give his comments on everyone's performance. Surely, he was as kind as his meager salary allowed him to be.

But to me? No. His words burned a hole in my chest the size of a script.

"Dismissed. Go to your friends and families, I'm sure they'd all like to congratulate you in person," were the next words I managed to catch leave the man's lips.

I stood still.

As she left, Thea gently slapped my back. I knew she'd forgiven me, but it took me far longer to forgive myself. In fact, I don't know if I really ever did.

My parents and brothers had seats in the back; despite their easy-to-recognize appearance, they prefer to stay lost in the crowd. They all (yes, even Des) clapped as I walked over, still in costume. My father noticed the smeared lines of stage makeup down my cheeks first but chalked it up to the stage lights making me sweat it off. I've always been his tough little girl, not much of a crier, in his mind at least. Perhaps I just never let him see me so vulnerable.

"I think someone is waiting to greet you," my mother said in a singsong way. I could only guess who she was talking about and, as I spun around only for my gaze to meet his chest, my guess was proven correct.

Beckett had clearly put some time and effort into his appearance that night. His mop of a head of hair was combed for once, slicked back with god knows how much gel, and his shirt had only the slightest of noticeable wrinkles in it. The glow in the dark shoelaces were a nice touch, they must have made it easy for others to avoid stepping on his skis-for-feet as they left their aisles.

"Great job up there," Beckett grinned his gap-toothed grin, keeping his hands behind his back until the final sound left his lips, upon which he produced the most ridiculous bouquet I'd ever seen.

"Gee, grocery store carnations, every girl's dream," I muttered.

I must have cracked a small smile because his grin got wider, and he went in for the hug. I did not return it; I did, however, take the flowers.

"It really was a great show, just great," Beckett said when he finally released me. My parents had stepped away and dragged my brothers with them. Sometimes parents do have common sense.

"As great as your vocabulary, I'm sure."

His eyebrows wavered as did his grin. I was sure I'd cut him down a peg until he spoke.

"Have you been…crying?"

I choked. "What? No. Don't be ridiculous." I wanted to sneak away but my family was nowhere to be seen. Instead, I did what absolutely no rational person would do: I went for the door.

He followed.

Not only did he follow, he followed all the way through campus, wordless until eventually, he took a seat beside me on the bleachers by the track field.

"Were you?" he broke the thick night air with his words. I picked petals off the flower for a few moments more before nodding once, half-hoping he wouldn't see.

"Why?"

"Because, Bucket," my voice crackled like lightning, "I saw you. Why did you even come? You ruined everything, just like you always do."

"What? What are you talking about?" He looked hurt, but no more hurt than he looked when I normally spoke to him. More surprisingly, he stood his ground by standing up, offering me a hand as he did.

I looked up at his dichromatic eyes, surprised by how much they glimmered like stars in that very moment, and took his hand out of sheer instinct.

"It doesn't matter," Beckett said as he squeezed my hand. His palm was sweaty and made me pull away. He released me once more. "It doesn't matter why, it just matters. Let's get you fixed up. Go change and meet me at your car."

I arched a brow.

He flushed red. "No, nothing weird, trust me. You trust me, right?" He tried to run his fingers through his hair but got caught in the gel-entangled net. I laughed and that must have set him at ease. It sure did for me.

"Only as far as I can throw you."

⁓

"Roast? Why are we going there? It's closed," I said as I drove.

Beckett didn't even reply. Instead, he simply swung a ring of keys around his finger and grinned his shit-eating grin.

"You really must want to lose your job," I said with a smirk.

"You're worth it," I could have sworn he'd said, but the sound of my tires on gravel muffled the sound as I pulled into the parking lot and parked in my usual spot. Maybe he said it, maybe I just needed to hear it.

As we stepped out of the car and up to the door, Beckett tripped over the cemented boundary between sidewalk and parking lot. I, once more, could not hold back a laugh. "Okay, so you haven't had the best of days, well I'm going to fix that."

He flung open the door and turned on the lights to the old shop that filled so many of my memories. "Okay, sure, how?" I asked incredulously. He grabbed my hands and tugged me inside, all the way to behind the counter. I'd never been behind the counter.

It was strange seeing everything how he must've seen it. He started setting out whipped cream canisters and chocolate syrup bottles as I looked out on a place that was so familiar to me from this new vantage point. Suddenly, all at once, it had become unfamiliar.

"It's time to become a barista," he grinned, motioning to the plethora of coffee-making accoutrements before me.

"What?" I laughed, already reaching for the whipped cream. I'd always wanted to use one of the fancy coffee shop canisters anyway, so why not, I thought.

Working together we created one of the most absurd concoctions to ever exit those doors and, let me remind you, the Volatile was a thing. Chocolate shavings galore, something more akin to a milkshake than a coffee, the Rainy Jane was born, and, to this day, I can only picture the drink as an image of it in Beckett's hands, whipped cream adorning his nose like a crown on the head of a king.

CHAPTER 11

Nothing to a Dress

For the first time in a long time, I found myself in a dress. No, not a little black dress, nothing like that. Well, at least not in connotation, I suppose what I was wearing would be considered a little black dress, when I think about it. But that's neither here nor there.

The point is, I was wearing a dress. Not a black tank top and running shorts, not a flannel and some ripped jeans, but a dress. Now, Jane, you must be asking, why does this matter?

Well, fact of the matter is that my experience with dresses is rather slim. I wore a dress and a godforsaken corset on stage as Juliet, I wore a dress to my grandfather's funeral, and I wore a dress to prom. I am somewhat glad to say that this dress-wearing collegiate experience was more similar to the latter, not the prior two.

A formal award ceremony was being held by my department for those high achieving students who have no lives. I happened to be one of those unlucky souls, at least at that point. Making friends in college was somewhat of a challenge, especially in such a career track as mine. When it comes to acting, it will always be a competition. Whoever gets the lead role is everyone's worst enemy and, in the first, albeit wholly insignificant, production of the year, guess who was chosen?

I often found myself envious of my understudy. All the talent of the lead but none of the hate and scorn directed at her. She sure had plenty to direct towards me, though, in as petty a manner as one could imagine.

~

You may be wondering where I could go from here. The season of *Romeo and Juliet* had ended, so should this story, right? Well, I suppose it could. It could if life were simpler if life bookended itself as nicely as that. I like to think of my story as one fit for a proper ending. Even after the death of its namesakes, the play continued for just a little while longer, giving life to a world without them. To tell this story how it should be told, I must do the same.

But anyway, I was invited to what was meant to be a prestigious event but instead was just a pathetic reason to get out of my dorm on a Saturday night. As I stepped into the black box theatre they were using to host the first year's award ceremony, I felt a slip of paper slide between my fingers. The night's itinerary was warm, clearly fresh off the printer. The heat of the paper pulled me back to a time well worth remembering.

~

"You'll never guess what I got my hands on," Thea beamed as she slipped an envelope into my hand. Heat radiated from it. Whatever was inside, I could tell it had come fresh off the printer.

"Well, considering how excited you are, it must be something pretty great," I said, deadpanned as usual. It didn't seem worth the effort to feign excitement; Thea had plenty for the two of us.

It's strange, looking back on it, to think that two years had passed by that point since that very first production. More had come and passed, sure, but none were as memorable in my mind. I guess the first always leaves a certain taste on your tongue.

It doesn't seem like much time had passed between the final curtain call and Thea slipping that warm envelope between my fingers, but I suppose a child's concept of time is skewed. My father would always say that high school would be done and over with before I even knew it and, low and behold, he was right. I can only begin to imagine how college will be the same way.

But that's not the point of this story. The point is that Thea was excited about something, and I was there to witness it.

"Someone's extra bouncy today, what's the big news?" a familiar voice called out as he sauntered into our, thank the shining stars, joint senior homeroom classroom. Eddie wrapped an arm around Thea's shoulders, putting a halt to her excited hopping but not wiping the beaming smile off her face.

"Oh! I got one for you too, don't worry," she said as she handed him an envelope.

Victor and Valerie walked in just as Eddie began to break the seal.

"What's all the fuss about?" Valerie asked as she hopped up on my desk, taking a seat atop it. Victor did the same with Thea's and the two of them blocked the hallway by holding hands. They had put an end to their volatile relationship and instead chose to focus on themselves for a year, eventually drifting back together. I'm certain it couldn't have hurt that Valerie was Victor's little sister Victoria's babysitter, yes it ended up being a girl. I suppose that's one of the benefits of telling a story with a time skip, you get answers a little faster.

Thea slipped another envelope between the two of them, the same grin still adorning her face.

"Oh! Oh my! You didn't!" Eddie gasped as he opened the envelope, pulling out the paper inside.

"Alright, I'll bite," I sighed as I opened the envelope as well. To my surprise, the contents were nothing surprising. "You didn't…" I groaned.

"I did!"

"Wait. Why do I have two?" I arched a brow.

"Well…"

"Oh hell no."

"C'mon Jane, it's prom," Eddie chimed in.

Yes, each envelope had a fresh off the printer prom ticket or two inside. I was anything but thrilled. If you couldn't have guessed, prom isn't necessarily my scene. I'd convinced the gang to ditch it junior year, but I suppose I couldn't have it my way every time, regardless of how hard I tried. I remember how disappointed Thea was that I didn't want to go but I made it up to them by getting us all tickets to *Hamilton* with saved up birthday money. Those theatre geeks couldn't stay mad at me for long, especially not with all that built-up glee.

The rest of that period was spent gawking over dresses, coordinating outfits, getting an itinerary together, all stuff I kind of hate. I stayed out of it, for the most part, instead focusing my attention on the second ticket in my envelope.

～

A week had come and gone before any real news of prom had reached the rest of the school. Thea, working some of her witchcraft I suppose, had gotten us each a ticket a week early. While the rest of the school was busy buying tickets, my group was planning promposals. The first to go was the most ornate and, quite frankly, the most unexpected. It was stunning, in all reality, that it only took him a week of planning to get everything organized the way he did.

Then again, Edison Bishop is no slouch when it comes to the finer details or the finer things in life.

The day started as nonchalantly and casually as any day ever could. First period was there and by in a flash, as were all the other boring classes of the day, and then it finally came to theatre. I noticed it first, the change in atmosphere, but Thea remained oblivious as she stepped inside and took her seat. The second she sat down, the song began. What song, you ask? Well, what song could it be but riveting, sexually enchanting, absolute bop that is "Lay All Your Love on Me" by ABBA.

Once the song started playing, there was no stopping what was going to happen next and everyone knew it. Mitchell, who I hope was in on the whole thing, just sort of hung his head in defeated silence as Thea gasped and stood up on her desk. In came Eddie and the flashmob.

There were confetti cannons, there were balloons, which came out of Mitchell's office, there were posters galore. It was the perfect promposal by all means, it was just unexpected, at least to me. Thea danced along, learning the choreography as they went along. Finally, at the end of the song, Eddie and Thea were face to face and, from behind him dropped down a sign which had been rolled with glitter so there was a glitter explosion to serve as the backdrop. "Don't go wasting your emotions, just go to prom with me," the sign read and Eddie sang along.

The entire flash mob had surrounded them by this point, pointing and waiting for an answer. That was the moment when I questioned why I knew nothing about this whole event. Then I realized I am no good at keeping secrets, especially when it comes to T. She just gets so excited whenever she can tell I'm keeping a secret and she drags it out of me. I couldn't be mad that Eddie kept it a secret from her, though I was a little pissed when I noticed Valerie and Victor holding confetti cannons, waiting patiently for the response of what seemed like the century.

"Eddie, you didn't," Thea started, the expression of a kid in a candy store plastered to her face.

"Nothing but the best for you," Eddie took one of her hands and kissed it, grinning from ear to ear. "Besides, we made a promise four years ago."

I remembered Thea telling me something about that freshman year before I knew all these chaotic people. Some theatre guy said they'd go to prom together senior year. When she asked him why, apparently, he'd said that while he'd never date a woman, if he had to, it'd be T. I, unlike T, didn't know whether or not that was a compliment. Apparently, I later learned, it was a major one.

"Edison Bishop," she began.

"Thea Alderson," he retorted.

"It would be my pleasure to go to prom with you." She beamed that beautiful Thea smile of hers and everyone cheered. Victor and Valerie popped off their confetti cannons. Even Mitchell couldn't help but crack a bit of a grin at it all.

Victor and Valerie had a much less showboating way of asking one another to prom, which was surprising given their very "center of attention" relationship within the theatre department.

They kept the whole thing rather private, so I only really know what they told me. I guess she was set to babysit one night when, in reality, Victor hijacked it and instead was going to surprise her. Little did he know, Valerie had already talked with his parents and explained her whole plan to them. She wanted him to be there so she could show up with his favorite pizza and a stack of movies to ask him to prom. He had a cake ordered and everything. Neither of them saw it coming but they had a lovely night, nonetheless.

In reality, I think this serves to show how good they were for each other after figuring themselves out. Sometimes people grow apart only to grow back together, and Vic and Val are the perfect example of that.

By that point, the group had already decided on a theme for our coordinated outfits because, yes, we were those kinds of friends. Rather than just find dresses we liked, we had to stick to a certain color scheme. Thea and Val decided on it, I decided not to fight it, so we each got assigned a Powerpuff Girl. I ended up as the blue one, whoever that is. I can't say I know much about this little sub-genre of nerd, but I do know that the blue one and I aren't exactly anything alike. I'd say we couldn't be friends, but, then again, I'm friends with Thea.

The girls and I decided, well they decided, and I decided not to fight it, on a day for shopping. Vic and Eddie said they'd go tux shopping and, had it not been for Eddie's obvious excitement, I'm not sure I would have believed them. If I was in their shoes, I would have said I was going and not gone, but alas, I'm the ride most of the time so, if plans are made, I am very much so expected to stick to them. And how can't I with Thea and Valerie's pouty faces staring at me, begging?

I did like I did just about every time they asked for anything; I caved.

Saturday morning at eight, because we needed to get there before all the good stuff was scoped out and selected. I didn't get what the big deal was, they tend to have more than one dress of any kind, what did it matter if we didn't get the first? Apparently, we had to confirm that we were the first in case anyone else picked the same dress. We weren't going to be caught copying anyone, whatever that meant.

It went exactly how you would imagine dress shopping with me would go. Thea and Valerie had a blast making me their dress-up doll and I dealt with it because I guess it was better than not having friends like them. By noon, yes noon, it did take us four hours, Thea and Valerie both had a dress in hand. I was the one making things difficult.

"C'mon J, just try this one on," Thea pleaded, holding a dress way too short and way too sparkly for my liking out to me.

"No, no, that's just not going to work, she'd like something more like this," Valerie said, pointing to something frilly and frankly atrocious.

Their arguing went on for a good while, which is probably why it took four hours to find a dress for me. As their bickering faded to the back of my mind, I drifted through the store, my hand running along the rows of different fabrics. Satin, silk, polyester, sure they feel different, but to me, they're all kind of the same. And then I stopped, something different beneath my fingers.

Mesh?!

I looked down, shocked for a moment until I saw a double-layered dress, dark blue and covered in constellations. No, not glitter, not sparkles, but actual constellations. The dress itself was short-sleeved but the mesh created these long and, in my mind, elegantly flowing sleeves down to the wrists. In the right light, which the clothing rack provided with its shadow to block out the overbearing florescence of any mall, it almost looked like each star glowed a little. I know it was chalked up to the contrast in color and lighting and whatnot but, at that moment, it felt as clichély magical as any girl discovering her prom dress could be.

"This one?" I asked, trying to maintain an air of nonchalance because, if those two knew I had any sort of interest in a dress, I'd never hear the end of it.

I wish I could say they looked thrilled, but they didn't. They looked hesitant at best, disgusted at worst.

And then I tried it on.

This was enough to quench their Jane in dress fantasies. The dress was a little more form-fitting than I think I would've preferred on any other day but, for some reason, I was fine with it. The two gawked and squealed. I rolled my eyes. Everything was as would be expected.

Dresses in hand, receipts in bags, we made our way to the food court for a shitty mall lunch and, post shitty mall lunch, decided to meet the boys back at Roast.

They had been there for hours.

When the little bell above the door rang, the mood shifted entirely, or at least the focus of the mood did. Rather than be a girl's day, it became a day of theatre geeks with just the simple sound of the bell. To our surprise, our drinks were already made but not too long ago. They were made at just the right time so when we walked through the door, they wouldn't be getting cold or watered down. Beckett was really good at what he did, even I have to admit that.

"Hey! Look who finally showed up," Eddie teased, a whipped cream mustache making him look both older and younger at the same time.

"Welcome in," Beckett said rolling his eyes. He had to say it every time someone entered the shop so, when it was just us, he was pretty sick of it.

"Yeah, yeah, we're fashionably late, big surprise," Valerie huffed as she plopped onto the couch beside Victor, who immediately wrapped his arm around her. I know, it was hard not to feel nauseous around them.

Thea grabbed her sugary, overly caffeinated beverage and sat down in one of the old armchairs, throwing her legs over the armrest as she blurted, "So, Jane, why don't you look at your drink?"

I could feel Beckett's cheeks begin to burn from behind the counter. I knew this was going to be a disaster. "Oh?" I arched a brow, grabbing my cup.

Written in the foam of my latte somewhat messily but clearly with intent and practice, was a single word and a single punctuation.

Prom?

Everyone stared at me with stars in their eyes except for Beckett, who was staring right at the ground. They all seemed to be waiting for a response, a gasp, a girly "Yay!" but, if you haven't gathered by now, I'm not quite the type to live up to those expectations. Instead, I couldn't help but snort.

"Are you asking me to *my* prom?"

Beckett burned a brighter red, which I didn't think was possible at that point. "I, uh, well, y-yes?"

Everyone's staring suddenly felt like daggers held to my back. I don't think my response was that mean, in all honesty. He didn't even go to our school.

I sighed. "Y'know Bucket, it would be kind of lame if we all went without you."

His gaze left the floor and shot up to meet mine in a startling instant. I couldn't help but flush a little bit. "So, is that a yes then?"

I waited a moment, mulling it over. I had to admit, I liked the promposal. It was simple, sweet, not outlandish or showboaty, not private and unnecessarily awkward. It's not like I had guys knocking down my door to ask me, either. Plus, I meant what I said; it would've been lame to leave him behind.

"Sure."

That's when I stopped liking the promposal because everyone in the shop started cheering and hollering. Not just my friends, but other random customers. It seemed like the whole place was in on it. I didn't like that, but like I did with most things that day, I grinned and bared it.

～

"Oh, Jane! You look beautiful!" my mother gasped as I came out of my room, all dolled up for prom, thanks to Thea and Valerie.

I felt like a clown.

I wasn't a girl who was into makeup. I dealt with it for the stage, sure, but that was supposed to be ridiculous looking, unlike all make-up which I think looks ridiculous but isn't really supposed to. The dress felt way more revealing wearing it then than it had in the store, but I guess that was because there were more eyes to be revealed to. I was being seen and I wasn't a fan.

"Thank you, thank you, it was tough work, I'll admit. But damn, did I work some magic,' Thea beamed. Valerie elbowed her. "Okay, okay, did *we* work some magic." She had to smack my hand at that point because I kept messing with the false lashes they put on me. I remember they had to take a five-minute laughing break after I asked, concerned if the glue was going to rip off my actual eyelashes.

I shuffled awkwardly as my mother complimented and praised the two of them. They both looked gorgeous, I'll be the first to admit, but I just didn't feel like I was in the same category, let alone anywhere near it.

"What's on your face?" Desmond snarked as he walked out of the bathroom, not even trying to hide how aghast my appearance had made him.

"Des," my mother began.

"I think she looks great," Norman smiled as he headed towards the couch, turning to Desmond, "But then again, you wouldn't know what a girl's supposed to look like. None will come within fifty feet of you."

That comment was enough to put an immediate start to a brawl to the death. My father eventually put a halt to it, dragging the two of them to his office so they could work out their feelings with a professional, something they looked just absolutely thrilled to have to do.

My mother began taking photo after photo of the three of us, eventually asking us to go pose in the front yard. As I opened the front door and stepped out, I was quickly met with an obstacle; Beckett was standing there, corsage in one hand, the other reaching for the door. He was early and, by the looks of it, a little sweaty.

"Oh, uh, hey, this is for you," he said as he shoved the box with the corsage into my hands. His sleeve brushed up against my wrists because they were just a tad too wide while somehow also a tad too short and the tuxedo itself was just a tad too big. I could only imagine how hard it was to find something that even remotely fit his weird and lanky frame.

"Whoa, he beat us here!" I heard Victor call out as Eddie locked his new car. When I say new, I mean it, his parents were loaded and he was spoiled. But, whatever, it's not like I was jealous of him or anything. Even though Eddie always had cash to burn, I could have sworn I saw an exchange of money between a very disgruntled Victor and a very pleased with himself Eddie but what do I know.

"Thanks, I guess," I said as I took the corsage out of the box and slipped it onto my wrist. Even I have to admit, it was lovely, even if I was a bit of an asshole about it in the moment.

Eddie and Vic each put an arm around Beckett as they walked up to the door, all of them together looking like the Rowdy Ruff Boys. "You clean up well, sir. And you, Jane, look like a star," Eddie waved a hand mystically as if casting some kind of spell.

In my mind, it must've been a sleep spell because I was exhausted by that point.

"Look at you boys!" Valerie exclaimed as she came around the corner, running over and wrapping her arms around Victor.

"Mister Bishop," Thea gave Eddie a curtsey.

"Miss Alderson," he retorted with a bow. They both laughed and started to gawk at each other's appearance and then together at mine.

Someone else already had that covered though. Beckett's dichromatic eyes were glued to me. I snapped in front of his gaze, a brow arched, and lips pursed. "You got something to say?"

He startled a bit, "Oh, yes, you look…amazing."

I tilted my head. "Little much?" I whispered.

Beckett shrugged in a teasing manner. Whatever was going on with him, he got over it pretty quickly once I broke the ice a bit.

I rolled my eyes.

My mother couldn't help but get an abundance of pictures before we left. I'm sure she'd filled up her memory card that night. Though, my favorite photo to come of it all was taken later in the night, not by my mother.

~~~

I'm still not sure why, to this day, I did it.

Prom itself was as much my thing as you could imagine. The punch was spiked early in the night and that was the only thing that got me through. That and the company wasn't half bad. The others were far more into the festivities, though. Dancing was never really my specialty and I learned very quickly that it wasn't Beckett's either.

"Could you please, for the love of all that is holy, watch where you're stepping?" I asked, exasperated, as Beckett's two left feet stepped on mine for the hundredth time.

He didn't take me seriously and started laughing. I remember that I was, in fact, very serious in the moment. I also remember going home that night with bruises covering the tops of my feet. "I'm sorry, I'm sorry, you just…do you ever have a good time?" he asked.

I blinked, stunned at the question. "What's that supposed to mean?"

"Oh, I dunno," Beckett smugly said, "You just never seem to be enjoying anything." He smirked playfully and his tone matched his facial expression but, damn, I felt more seen than I had felt even earlier that day and man did I hate it.

"Whatever," I huffed, stepping away from him and back towards our table at the venue. My school held prom in a big library, which is apparently strange as hell, from what I've heard of other peoples' prom experiences, and we'd managed to grab one of the few tables they had
~~~

scattered around the place. He followed, of course, like the puppy of a person he is.

"Want me to get you a drink?" he asked, still standing as I sat down.

"Sure."

He returned minutes later with a single glass.

"Where's yours?"

"Oh, uh, I forgot to get one for me."

I laughed the entire time he was gone getting himself a drink. I was laughing when he got back. I had laughed so hard I nearly cried but I refused to because my makeup would be ruined and, while I wouldn't have cared, Thea most certainly would've killed me. I continued to laugh at him up until he took his seat and begged me with his eyes to stop.

It took a few moments, but eventually, he broke the not so silent air.

"So..."

"Great start."

Beckett sighed heavily and leaned back in his chair, almost falling backward, causing me to start laughing again.

"How come you're only enjoying yourself when I'm making a fool of myself?" he asked.

"Well, cause it's funny, of course." I chugged the rest of my punch and stood up. "C'mon, we may as well explore the joint. Surely there has to be something better to do than just dance."

He shrugged and followed just as Thea and Eddie were being announced to be prom king and queen. No surprise there. The two were rather popular, for theatre kids at least, and everyone loves the token gay prom king.

"What's over there?" Beckett asked as we wandered. I shrugged and tugged him that way. In a secluded room, kind of out of the way, in all honesty, sat a single photo booth and a mess of props. It seemed like they had expected there to be a line for it but there wasn't. I couldn't help but chuckle at the sight of the pathetic thing. Then I made a suggestion. It was probably the alcohol talking. And before you start thinking, no it wasn't anything like that.

"Really?" Beckett asked.

"Sure, why not?" I shrugged as I started up the photo booth and got inside, motioning for him to follow. He did.

The first photo was casual, an arm around each other and normal smiles. The second was a bit goofier, funny faces and all. The third is my favorite from the night. Now, I cannot begin to tell you what compelled me to do this, but I kissed his cheek. In doing so, I caused him to blush the brightest red I have seen to this day. That photo alone was worth the whole hellscape of a night.

~~~

When I finally returned to my dorm after the event, from which I came back with a few awards, one in recognition of my high GPA and one for best monologue even though I knew my performance was nothing special, I cracked the window to let some of the cool night air in. I remember that stars looking especially bright that night, even if I didn't spend much time admiring them. I plopped down onto my bed, still in my dress; all I wanted to do was fall asleep. I'm pretty sure I did so staring at my desk, at a certain photo I had pinned to my pegboard.
~~~

CHAPTER 12

Seeing Stars

It was a class trip, one that we'd have to write a paper on later, but it was something I was excited for, nonetheless. I didn't get out much that first semester of college, and any chance to do so seemed like a blessing in disguise. I'd pretend to hate it, just as I did many things, but end up having a great time. Though, if there was even the slightest of reasons to cancel, you know I would.

With this, the only chance I had of getting out of it was if the professor canceled and that was not going to happen. He'd been talking about it for the better part of a month, how he got us all tickets to see a production of *Into the Woods* at the Pantages. He wanted us to see what acting on the stage as a career was really like and just so happened to be friends with the director of said production. He got to see an old friend, we got real-life experience, and we all got to support the arts. Overall, it was a win-win.

As I walked up to the theatre and saw a huddle of my classmates, the only thing I could think about is how much I had always wanted to play Cinderella and how desperately I wished Mitchell would have chosen this particular musical for one of our seasons. It was a funny thing for me to wish, considering I barely ever sang, especially not onstage, but the wishes of children tend to be foolish.

My mind then drifted to the last time I had heard the soundtrack for *Into the Woods*, recalling the belting voices and, quite frankly, stunning performances of Eddie and Thea as I drove them, yes, into the woods. Victor and Valerie occasionally joined in, and I couldn't help myself when it came to "The Last Midnight" but our friend kept his gap-toothed mouth shut and his dichromatic gaze glued to the trees.

~

"I can't believe we're doing this," Beckett said when he finally had to courage to speak in that car filled with chaos.

"What was that? I can't hear you over the dogs barking," Valerie teased our choir, who both responded, feigning offense.

"It is pretty crazy, huh? And of all the senior ditch days to plan, you planned a camping trip?" I glanced in the mirror back at Thea. She was in the middle with Eddie and Vic and Val were spooning in the back of the endlessly spacious minivan. Beckett sat up front and controlled the music. He was a pretty good road trip DJ.

"I strive to be unexpected," Thea grinned as she bit a hunk off a licorice rope.

"Yeah, I guess I never took you much for the camping type, Thea," Beckett turned the music down a bit so everyone could speak and hear. I knew Thea was big into camping, but I had expected something a little crazier from her in all honesty. This seemed, if anything, a little pedestrian.

"What? Am I too pretty a princess for the woods?" she arched a brow. Beckett immediately retreated from the conversation, ashamed of his once-biased view of her.

Valerie sat forward, leaning in between Eddie and Thea, "I think it's a perfect way to cap off the years. In the middle of nowhere, with no clue what we're doing? It's poetic." We all laughed, except for Beckett who was still trying to cleanse the red from his cheeks. He sure was easy to embarrass.

"Cunningham hardly counts as the middle of nowhere but point taken. I respect the sentiment," Thea gave a single, self-assured nod.

Val shrugged. "Eh, potato, potahto."

"What's the big surprise you've been saving up, anyway? You did say you'd tell us on the way to the campsite and we're getting pretty close now," Victor piped up as he rested his chin atop Valerie's head.

"Well, I'm glad you asked," Thea reached into the front pocket of her backpack, which she insisted on keeping on her lap throughout the ride. Out came a bag of peach rings, yes that multicolored sugar-coated candy. I didn't get it at first. Everyone else did.

"Thea, you didn't," Eddie gasped, a smile spreading across his lips.

"You bet I did."

I arched a brow into the rearview mirror. While he was easy to embarrass, he was rather good at saving others from the same fate so Beckett whispered just to me, "They're edibles."

"Oh shit," I chuckled, "So, you were just not going to tell me you brought drugs into my car?"

Thea giggled as if she'd already taken one. "Oh hush."

I shrugged a shoulder. I recalled that, as I left to pick everyone up, my parents gave me two instructions: no drugs, no sex. At the time, I just thought it was funny that they left out drinking but I'm sure they knew that a bunch of kids going into the woods could only end up being any fun in so many ways. But then I remembered that I was 18 and their instructions drifted to the deepest, darkest pits of my mind, never to be found again.

"Where did you even get those?" Victor asked.

"My dad's got a stash; these are supposed to be medicinal so they're really strong. I snagged one for each of us. He probably won't even notice."

Everyone in the car hooted and hollered, Beckett and I a little less so. It seemed we were the most hesitant two. In a strange way, it reassured me to know that there was someone else who wasn't fully comfortable with the idea but who was also just kind of along for the ride.

About twenty minutes of questions, answers, and karaoke came and went before we finally arrived at the campsite. Minivans aren't necessarily made for off-roading, so the drive was a little precarious at times, but we made it safe and sound. Everyone did their part when it came to unpacking and getting everything set up.

Thea and Beckett, the two with the most camping experience out of all of us, set up the tents. I immediately started unloading the food and booze into the bear-resistant container the campsite had. Eddie, who we learned during that trip is a bit of pyro, took to getting a fire-pit set up. Victor and Valerie split up for once and unloaded bags into everyone's tents.

There were three total so the plan was that Victor and Valerie would take one, Thea and I another, and Eddie and Beckett the last. That was the plan. Edibles and plans do not mix well.

The time it took us to get everything settled was also spent shouting what we wanted to spend the day doing. Having left early in the morning, we had most of the day ahead of us. The Houck Area had plenty for us to do and we wanted to do it all.

We ended up deciding on starting our trip with a hike to avoid the hotter midday weather and then when that weather did arrive, we'd go swimming at the lake. Whenever it got too dark or cold, we'd then roast marshmallows on the fire maintained by our resident pyro and whoever decided to indulge would take a peach ring. Once everything was set up, we threw on our hiking shoes, which for most of us were just beat-up old sneakers and headed out to find a trail.

"We're definitely going all the way to the falls so be sure to bring water and everything, it's not going to be a short jaunt," Thea directed the group, falling into the role of leader with the same grace and ease she always seemed to possess.

"Yes ma'am," Eddie saluted from the ground as his free hand held his laces tight. He and Thea were the ones with hiking boots and that, in our minds, made them the immediate candidates for any sort of leadership role. With Thea already having taken command, Eddie was expected to fall in line as her second. The rest of us were newbs, just ready for the ride.

The hike was arduous, and the sun shone bright, though Thea had made sure each of us was lathered in sunscreen and bug spray galore, so it posed little issue aside from sheer heat. The trail wasn't narrow by any means, but it was only wide enough for two people to be side by side. With Thea and Eddie leading our small platoon and Victor and Valarie being as inseparable as always, Beckett and I ended up helming the rear.

The two chatterboxes at the front pretended they were tour guides, giving the rest of us a rundown of the area and the foliage. Though, in all honesty, with Eddie's brief boy scout experience and Thea's family history of trips to the Houck, the tour was more than sufficient, even as tuned out as it was by the chatter of the other hikers. Beckett and I paid what attention we could but most of the way up was a chorus of my laughter as he tripped and Thea asking if Beckett needed more sunscreen because he seemed to burn up.

"Alright, it's about to get pretty steep here so watch your steps. Yes, Beckett, I'm speaking directly to you," Thea whipped two fingers in his directions, letting him know her eyes were on him, "I won't have any scuffed knees or scraped elbows on my watch, alright?"

His steps after that callout were more surefooted so my entertainment during the hike suddenly vanished. My thoughts wandered through the branches and leaves as we plowed our way up the trail and finally to the falls. The view was worth the hour we spent trying to get to it.

To me, the falls seemed as magnificent as the Niagara. To anyone who'd actually seen any of the world, they were a minor beauty in comparison, still something to behold but with far less astonishment. When I glanced over the group to gauge their expressions, Thea and Eddie just looked glad to have made it, Victor and Valarie were looking at each other, and Beckett, to my surprise, seemed as enraptured by the view as I had been upon first sight.

"Pretty cool, huh?" I asked him.

"Very," he tore his gaze from the falls to meet mine, "I've never really been camping or seen anything like this."

I had to pause at the amazement in his eyes as it was infectious, forcing me to turn away and back to the falls. When I spoke, my voice seemed swallowed by the, in my mind, thunderous downfall of the water that was probably nothing more than a trickle.

"Me neither."

～

The hike down was as uneventful as the hike up, though we all spoke of how excited we were to get in the water. The heat was starting to really kick in and we were all feeling it. The sweat dripping down into my old Converse was getting old, so even I was excited in some capacity.

Once we arrived back at the campsite, it was a quick series of actions until we were making our way to the lake. Changing into swimsuits, grabbing our cooler full of sandwich supplies so we were ready for lunch, gathering towels and chairs and anything we could possibly think we'd need. Thea was sure to grab the first aid kit, a worrywart like her wasn't just going to leave that behind, and we girls ended up making the guys carry most of our supplies. I was saddled with only my fold-out chair and the sketchbook I opted to bring along.

One thing you should know about me is that I'm not much a fan of water, not in the swimming capacity at least. I leave all that to Des, he's a swimmer enough for the both of us. It's not that I can't swim or anything, I just prefer not to get wet. My excitement for the lake came from the fact that there would undoubtedly be a breeze that came along with it, a bit cooler than the stagnant air of our hike.

By the time we made it to the lake we were already soaked, just by sweat. Everyone was ready to run right in, so I took it upon myself to offer to set up our lakeside hangout spot. I was immediately taken up on my offer as Thea handed me her chair and sprinted into the water, followed by Eddie who set the cooler down at my feet.

"Are you sure you don't want help?" Valerie asked, looking between me and the water with longing in her eyes.

"I'm sure, go have fun," I waved her off, already folding out chair after chair.

She and Victor nodded and ran off as well, leaving me and, for some reason, Beckett.

I didn't even look up from my task. "Aren't you going to swim?"

"Honestly," he began, grabbing a chair and folding it out, "I'm not much of a swimmer." He then held up the book in his hand, which I hadn't bothered to notice him bringing as we left the campsite. "I might walk in and get my feet wet but I don't plan on going much further than that." He kept helping with setup, turning his attention to the cooler. "You hungry?"

I shook my head, taking a seat in my chair once all the others were set up with towels draped over the arms for when the swimmers returned. Grabbing the sketchbook, I opened to a random page and started doodling.

Beckett arched a brow but took a seat as well and started reading. The quiet was nice, aside from the inevitable hollering from our swimming friends who would probably be playing a game of chicken if we'd bothered to look up. Instead, we sat together in the absence of conversation, him reading and me doodling, both keeping our minds busy.

Eventually, Beckett closed his book and stood up. He walked closer to the water but not close enough to get in. Instead, he knelt and started sifting through the sand. He piqued my curiosity so, after a few moments of consideration, I walked over, arms crossed, and head tilted.

"You ever skipped a stone?" he glanced up at me, one hand blocking the sun from his eyes, a goofy and childish grin on his face. His free hand cupped a small handful of smooth, flat stones.

I shook my head, wordless.

In an instant, my hand was filled with these stones and Beckett was standing beside me. "Okay, so what you're going to do is…" I tuned most of what he said out because I was still wondering how the hell my hand was full of stones so fast.

"…And boom," he effortlessly skipped a stone roughly five times across the lake before it sank into the water, "That's how you do it. Give it a try."

"What? No," I shook my head, "Not a chance."

"Why not? Scared to embarrass yourself?" he asked.

I tilted my head, frustrated by the remark. I took one of the stones from my left hand into my dominant one and reeled back, channeling everything into this toss. I squatted down close to the surface of the water, hoping that would make the toss easier to land. Instead, it just meant that I got a splash of water in my face when I threw the stone straight down into the water with a resounding sploosh.

It was finally Beckett's turn to laugh at me and boy did he take it. He was doubled over, clutching his stomach in a matter of seconds he'd laughed so hard. It took him over a minute to catch his breath, all the while I was scowling.

"Okay, okay, that was…certainly a first attempt," he chuckled as he spoke, "how about I help you?"

"Sure, Mr. Stone Skipping Expert. I'll gladly take whatever knowledge you can grant," I sighed and rolled my eyes, which widened when his arms wrapped around me, one hand on each of my wrists.

"Alright, so you've gotta pick a stone like this one, nice and flat," Beckett said, his head above mine as he guided my arms. "And you'll want to hold it like this, thumb here…" Once again, I felt unable to pay attention to his instruction but for an entirely different reason. We were so close I could smell his cologne. We hadn't even danced this close at prom, so I was taken aback, with good reason to be so I think. Together, our arms flung the stone at the water's surface, spinning just enough to skip right off again and again and again.

"Three skips, not bad," Beckett grinned, tilting his head as he released me. "Now, give it another go, I think you've got this now." I was busy praying he didn't notice the flush to my cheeks and thinking of excuses. The sun, surely I was getting heatstroke or something.

"O-okay, sure, I'll give it a shot," I shrugged a shoulder, taking a step away from him. I remembered the feeling of his body against mine and mimicked the steps he walked me through, winding up and releasing the stone at just the right moment. One skip was all I managed but I was pretty proud of myself, so much so that I gasped and beamed. "Ha! I did it!"

"You did it!" he exclaimed back, clearly thrilled. "Though, it was all thanks to me, a great teacher."

"Uh-huh, yeah, it was all you," I scoffed, picking up another stone and giving it another go. This one splooshed in the water. "Okay, maybe it was you," I caved.

We started competing, trying to see who could find the best stone and make the best throw. Eventually, I managed two skips but that was only once, and it was truly the best I had in me. Beckett got up to eight. There was no arguing, he was clearly better. Though I would never say it, especially not when he had a stupid shit-eating grin on his face that showed he knew it.

"What are you guys doing?" Thea called over as she got out of the water, heading to our set up.

"Well Jane over here would say losing, but I, on the other hand, am winning," Beckett chimed as he jogged back over.

"Whatever," I groaned, taking my sweet time to head back.

Victor looked up from the sandwich he was making, "C'mon now Jane, don't get lazy with the retorts. Those are one of your biggest strengths." He then handed the finished sandwich to Valarie, who happily began eating.

We all ate a nice lunch and hung out by the lake until the sun started setting, which honestly wasn't long after we'd arrived. The hike took up a good part of our day. Once we'd finished up our lakeside hijinks, which luckily did not involve dragging me into the water, we headed back to the campsite, still making the boys carry most of the cargo.

Immediately upon return, Eddie got a fire started.

"Good going Eddie," Thea said as she grabbed the marshmallows and a couple of sticks to roast them on, handing each of us one.

"Isn't this unsanitary?" Valarie asked, causing Eddie and Thea to boo her.

"It's camping, get used to it," they said in unison.

And get used to it we did. We were roasting marshmallows in a matter of minutes. Thea preferred hers perfect crispy golden, but Eddie was more of a flambe type. Victor, Valerie, Beckett, and I were something in between. After a while of talking shit and roasting each other as well as marshmallows, Thea pulled out the little baggie of peach rings once again.

"Alright, who wants one?" she asked, waving it around. Quickly, everyone's hands went up except for mine and Beckett's.

"Oh, c'mon you two, don't you want to try?" Valarie asked, though she quickly added, "No pressure if you don't."

"Yeah, no pressure, just know that if you want to, you're good to go," Eddie said.

"Every group needs a sober friend," Beckett said.

Victor turned to me. "Alright Jane, what's your excuse?"

"I don't think I need one, I'm just not really into it," I said. This attitude vanished the second I went to university, but that's probably because I found out it could make me less anxious. Though, at that time, I probably could have used it.

"Alright, don't peer pressure the girl, she said no," Thea said and turned her attention to me, "If you change your mind, they'll be in my pocket." She winked.

It took some time but, after forty minutes, Beckett and I were very suddenly the only coherent people at the site. They were laughing like they'd never laughed before, and we were stuck playing babysitters. I didn't regret my choice to stay sober at the time; I'd always been one of the more responsible ones of them all anyway. I could tell Beckett seemed a little bummed at the newly assigned group dad role he was thrust into.

We spent most of the night keeping them from getting too close to the fire. That was a big one. Another was keeping them from going back to the lake. They kept saying how much they wanted to swim but Beckett and I weren't exactly the best lifeguards, so we had to shoot down their requests.

We weren't all bad, though. We were sure to keep the snacks coming and the conversations rolling.

"What do I wanna be when I'm an actual adult?" Thea repeated my question, looking up at the stars and trying to reach them, "I wanna be one of those." She pointed at the sky, "A star."

We all laughed but knew what she meant. In some way, we all wanted to be stars in our own rights. I think the others took it to mean they'd shine brightly and be noticeable. I took it differently, though. I never wanted to be the center of attention, I know it's weird for an actor to say so, but it's true. An individual star, could you think of anything more overlooked? Who stares at a single star? No one.

And then I looked over at Beckett, who seemed to be doing just that. "That's the North Star," he said, pointing up at the sky, taking note of a single star.

Everyone oohed and awed at his astronomical knowledge. I was more impressed how he could pick it out. I know it's supposed to shine the brightest, but I mean, really, how much brighter than other stars can a star shine? Not enough for me to notice, I'll tell you that.

It was well into the night when everyone decided to hit the sack. The one thing Thea and the others learned is that the medicinal stuff tends to make you tired so they slept like rocks, which was unfortunate for me because Eddie had snuck into my tent and crashed in there. By the time I'd finished helping Vic and Val get settled, he and Thea were beyond waking.

"I can sleep outside," Beckett offered when he realized our situation.

I shook my head, "No need. C'mon." I held the flap to our tent open.

Unlike the others, who fell asleep with ease, Beckett and I were wide awake. We hadn't exhausted ourselves by swimming or with the peach rings, so we were stuck staring at either wall of the tent for a while before he spoke.

"Can't fall asleep?" he asked, his breath almost manifesting in the cool night air.

"Nope."

Silence overtook us once more.

"It's kind of weird," Beckett broke the still air once more.

"Hm?" I glanced over at him.

"We've all graduated, you guys are off to college, I'm just gonna be at the shop but my best customers will all be gone." There was a sadness to his tone, but also a bit of pride.

"Well, it's not like you won't hear from us. Besides, you'll be busy with community college classes," I tried.

"Yeah, you're right. I don't know."

"You don't know what?"

"I've just…" he paused, thinking about his next choice of words very carefully. There was something vulnerable about him, more than I'd seen before. I felt compelled to do something about it, so I did. Before he finished thinking about what to say, my lips were pressed against his. When I pulled away, his eyes were wide and his face was so stupid I had to force down laughter.

"You've just what?" I continued the conversation as if nothing had happened.

Beckett stammered and his burning red cheeks mixed with his endless array of freckles to make his face look like an impossible sunset.

I can't tell you what compelled me to say what I said next as even I don't know what it was, but I don't regret it. Perhaps I thought of this night as the end of an era, the end before something even began so I said it.

"I don't want to go to college a virgin."

Beckett looked incredulous. There was a thick cloud of silence that kept him from speaking anything other than the word, "O-oh?"

"You know that was your cue to fuck me, right?"

~

After an early breakfast and cleanup, we packed up the car with the groggiest of campers. Thea, Eddie, Victor, and Valarie all protested and begged that we let them sleep in. We'd paid for the campsite only for the day and would've been charged if we didn't leave so I couldn't allow it.

As I drove and the others slept, there was one thing keeping me wide awake and that was Beckett's hand on my knee.

CHAPTER 13

The End of the Beginning

Finals went by in a flash and suddenly I was on a flight home. My grades were nothing to celebrate, but winter break was enough to make me want to buy out Party City's confetti cannon supply. I'd get to see my family, I'd get to see my cat, I'd get to see my friend. I would basically get to do everything I didn't get to do during the semester, that is to say, I would get to enjoy living.

If there was one thing I learned from my first semester in college, it was that I had surely peaked in high school. I mean, come on, I was miserable, all things considered. My roommate, who made it very clear that she did not want to be friends, was even getting concerned by the end of it. I can't even blame her.

During finals week I found myself hitting the lowest low in a long time. I wish I was joking when I said this, but I survived for the entire week on nothing but a frosting-less chocolate sheet cake. Why you may ask? Well, I had decided that I would use all the time we were given to study and complete projects and write papers to do something I considered to be the exact opposite: binge the entirety of *Game of Thrones*. Why did I do this? Because my life was falling apart, why else?

I thought things would get better when I got home. I thought I'd see my friends, that they'd have missed me as much as I missed them. I thought I'd slip back into the life I had left behind.

I was wrong.

~

As I rode the escalator down to the pickup zone, I imagined all the faces that would be happy to see me. I was the last of us to get back, I told them the day and the time and even though they didn't respond, I thought that maybe, just maybe, they were planning a big surprise for me. That's what friends do, right? Well, I can't say I was disappointed when I saw my mom's face in the crowd, but I was a little disappointed to not see any other faces I recognized. There she was, my mother, my life-giver, all alone waiting for me.

I hurried down the escalator, struggling with my unwieldy suitcase the whole way down, and we embraced. She ran her fingers through the ends of my hair like she used to when I was little.

"I'm so glad you're home," she said.

I did my best not to tear up, "Me too."

The drive home was a lot of questions about how school was going. I kept my responses short because I didn't want her to worry. How are things? Good. How are classes? Good. Do you have a favorite professor? Not really. How were finals? Okay. Have you been eating well? Yeah. All the typical mom questions were pretty easy to shut down before things got too personal or depressing.

"Beckett came by the house today."

For the first time the whole car ride, I looked up from my phone. "What?"

"Yeah, he came by. I guess he got the time you were coming back confused. He said he wanted to be the first friend you saw when you got back." She glanced over in my direction, and we made eye contact for a brief second. Her look said everything you could imagine a mother's look would say when a boy came by the house looking for her daughter. It was infuriating.

I didn't say another word the whole ride home. Eventually, her smirk faded away.

～

I tossed my suitcase into the corner of my room and flopped down face-first onto my bed the second I could. Mr. Socks, not missing a beat, parked himself in the small of my back. I couldn't see him, but I knew he was comfortable, so I didn't dare to move. After all, it was nice to be missed but to also not be asked question after question about how horrible college was going.

I enjoyed the silence for all of the forty seconds it lasted before my door slammed open.

"Sis!" both Des and Nor said in unison before leaping onto my bed and startling Mr. Socks away. I'm sure one of them, if not both, had farted as they did so, just to annoy me even further.

"It's good to have you back," Norman said as he was the first to sit up and get off me. Desmond stayed a little longer before finally taking his place at the foot of my bed.

"You wanna go to lunch?" he asked, batting his eyelashes.

"Oh, you mean do I want to take you to lunch and pay for it, I'm assuming?" I grumbled into my comforter.

"Yes please," the unison returned.

I sighed heavily but shrugged. It wasn't like I had any plans for the day. I guess I could've told Beckett that I was actually back, but I honestly didn't feel like it. Lunch sounded good anyway. I hadn't eaten anything in the morning or on the flight. I'm a nervous flyer, believe it or not.

We hopped in the minivan, and I headed to their favorite spot. To me, it was just some old, decrepit diner, but to them, it was where Des went after every win at a swim meet, where Nor went after leading his team to victory in Science Olympiad, where they each had their first dates and first kisses. This was their theatre and, no matter how shitty I thought it was, I would indulge them and never tear down their sanctuary with my opinion.

They did their best to be mindful of mine when I had it at least.

"Order whatever you want, my treat," I huffed as I took a seat in the peeling pleather booth and leaned my elbow on the somehow constantly sticky table.

They both took what I said to heart. Burgers, fries, and shakes galore soon flooded our table. I shrugged off my slight annoyance because they were growing kids after all.

"So, what's it like?" Des asked through a mouthful of burger.

"Hm?"

"How's college?" Norman asked as he shoved a handful of fries in his mouth.

"Oh. Fine."

Desmond and Norman turned to each other and laughed. "That bad, huh?"

"What? It's not bad."

"Defensive already? Wow, didn't think it'd be this fast," Desmond smirked, "Let me guess, you're having a hard time making friends without Thea."

"I have plenty of friends."

"Yeah right. Remember when mom had us all share our locations with her? We can track you, y'know," Norman said as if it was something I should've known already.

"So what?"

"You're always in your room."

"We hang out in my room."

Norman arched a brow and Desmond choked on a sip of his milkshake to the point where it came out of his nose. I groaned and handed him a fistful of napkins and Norman laughed to the point where he was wheezing. I was just glad that the attention was off of me for even a moment. Regardless of how disgusting that moment was.

When things finally calmed down and all the snotshake was cleaned up off the table, the conversation picked up exactly where it left off, much to my disappointment.

"Have you heard from Thea? We figured you'd be too busy making plans with her to do anything with us so you agreeing to take us here was a bit of a shock," Norman said with the very same lack of tack he always had.

Desmond nodded in agreement, though I could see he elbowed our brother from beneath the table. He had a bit of a better understanding of people.

"We, uh, actually haven't talked in a while," I glanced down at the table but quickly added, "I'm sure she's just been busy."

"Oh, that's...weird," Norman swirled his straw and frowned slightly.

Neither of us believed me.

By the time I'd been home for almost a week, I was sick of not hearing from her. It may have been desperate but I made a choice. Her house was only a few down from mine, anyway.

It was strange. I couldn't remember the last time I had knocked on her door. Usually, I'd text her and she'd just come running down but after five minutes of standing there like an idiot staring at the unread message, my knuckles met wood.

As the door creaked open moments later, I was met with a familiar face. If only it had been Thea's.

"Oh, hello Jane," her father said, looking a little confused but otherwise the same as I'd always remembered him: tired.

"Is Thea here?" The words leapt out of my mouth. Even though I was mad at her, I was excited to see her.

"She didn't tell you?"

"Tell me what?"

"She decided to stay in LA over the break. Wanted to explore the city even more with her friends."

"Oh."

We stood there in silence, disappointment looming over the both of us like a thick fog. When his voice broke through, it echoed pity. "I can't believe she didn't tell you."

I shook my head as my shoulders quaked. "Me neither." Before he could feel any worse for me, I turned and left. I walked back to my house, fists clenched into tight balls, eyes welling with tears I would not let fall.

In retrospect, I should've felt bad for him and not myself. He was the one stuck spending the holidays alone.

〜

"Say cheese!" my father beamed as all of us siblings groaned and grumbled.

"Dad, we're not little kids anymore. Do we really have to keep doing this?" Desmond whined, motioning to the Christmas onesie he was stuck wearing. And then to the matching ones both Norman and I wore.

"As much as I love traditions, this is one I wouldn't mind watching die," Norman said.

"Not happening," the 'rents borrowed Norman and Desmond's trick of talking in unison.

"We have pictures of you kids like this ever since you were born. This tradition dies with us," my father said.

My mother couldn't help herself but add, "And you don't want that to be anytime soon, do you?"

We didn't stop grumbling but you bet your ass they got the picture they wanted. It certainly didn't hurt that Nor and Des were a little easier to convince once they realized the sooner we got it over with, the sooner they'd get to open their presents.

"Guys! You didn't!" Norman exclaimed as he opened his new set of test tubes.

"These are going to make the season so much easier," Desmond beamed as he slipped on the prescription swim goggles.

"Jane, honey, aren't you going to open yours?" my mother said after snapping a few pictures of their excited faces.

I shook myself out of my thoughts and sat up a little straighter. "Sure."

I tore the winter-themed, inclusive wrapping paper and revealed the reused Amazon box. "Wow, a box, thanks, guys. I've always wanted one of these," I couldn't help but be snide.

My mother rolled her eyes. "Open it," she said.

And I did.

〜

"Jane, honey, you okay?" my mother asked as she slowly opened my door, "You haven't come downstairs in a few days… Do you even know what day it is?"

It was New Year's Eve. I only knew because I saw Eddie's Instagram post about it. He was at some beach in Aruba with his parents. I also knew because I tried to make plans with Vic and Val but they were both busy.

"Uh-huh…" I mumbled into my pillow, pulling the covers over my head when she opened my curtains.

"Come on Jane, it's two, well past time to get up," she said as she laid down next to me. I could feel her arms wrap around me.

"I will."

"Nope. Now," she flung the covers off of me.

I groaned and sat up, staring at her incredulously. "Is this what you want?"

"It's a start. I'd also like it if you went and took a shower, got dressed, got ready for the day. But this is a start," she acknowledged. "Now come on, you've got an hour. Then I'm taking you to get a coffee."

"I don't want a coffee, mom."

"I don't care. Get up, get ready. I'll drag you there in your pajamas if I have to." She stood up and closed the door behind her as she left.

I contemplated going back to bed but knew better. She wasn't joking.

So I did what she said –got out of bed, took a shower, put on actual clothes, and headed downstairs. All within the hour time allotment given. An unimaginable feat, I know. I, too was rather proud of myself.

"Good, you're ready," my mother said as she snatched up her keys.

I nodded and headed out to the car, hopping into the front seat and buckling up without a word.

"You didn't have to run to the car, you know?" she chuckled.

"Couldn't be in the sunlight for too long."

She laughed as she started the car. I guess she thought I was kidding.

"I thought you'd be more excited to go to your favorite coffee shop."

"We're going to Roast?"

"Yes. Is that a problem?"

"Nope. No problem."

She sighed. "Look, I know I'm not Thea or Eddie or Victor or Valerie, but we can have fun together too?"

I don't think she realized how sad that sounded and I wasn't going to be the one to break it to her that I didn't want my only friend to be my mom.

Don't get me wrong, there's nothing wrong with being friends with your mom. Honestly, nowadays, I'd probably say that my mom's my best friend. But that isn't something you want to hear said about you, it's something you want to say for yourself. Someone else saying it makes it sound kind of sad. Saying it yourself makes it sweet.

"We can, mom," I couldn't help but sigh. The amount of pity in the car was starting to fog up the glass.

As we pulled up to Roast, I almost yelled at her. She parked in the wrong spot. She didn't even park in one of my backup spots, no, she just parked in some random spot. Like it didn't matter, but to me it did. And then I asked myself why it mattered. It's not like they were there. It's not like I could reminisce about pulling into that spot time and time again without getting sad. Without wondering why they didn't want to come there with me again. Without wondering why I was there with my mom instead of them. So I stopped myself. I didn't yell. I just got out of the car and headed to the door.

The bell rang above my head and I felt like I was back in high school the second it did. And then my mom walked in behind me and I felt like I was a child again. Friendless, clinging to my mother for all social interaction. Yeah. Not a good look.

"Jane?" I heard the voice behind the counter say before my eyes even had the chance to register the sight of the shop. Though, it's not like I really needed them to. I knew everything would be the same and, it was. The same ratty couches, the same beat-up chairs, the same cozy interior, and the same clumsy mess of a barista boy greeting me.

"Hey Bucket," I said.

A simple hello devolved into us making plans to hang out after he had gotten off his shift. I'm sure this was exactly what my mother wanted. In fact, she managed to vanish for the entirety of the conversation and somehow reappeared the moment I was ready to leave. Mothers are a special kind of magic.

We agreed that I would pick him up after his shift and, being indecisive young adults, we said we'd figure out what to do from there rather than making any concrete plans. There was something beautiful about the sky as I drove towards the Roast. The way sunlight clung to the sky, lingering for just a few moments more as the sun began to set and the shades of orange and pink turned purple and blue. Stars were just beginning to dapple their way through the atmosphere and reach my eyes. I saw the Roast. I saw the Roast go by.

I kept driving.

I wasn't sure where I was headed, my body taking over and doing the driving for me while I got lost in thought. It was as I sat at a stoplight, staring just above the glint of red that streaked off in all directions and formed a halo around itself, that I recalled a strange series of words that Thea said to me once.

I could see out of my peripheral that she was crying. She didn't want me to see so I pretended I didn't. It was one of the many nights she had spent at my house. She couldn't be home. I didn't prod.

She was curled on her side and the alarm clock shone the time in bright red on my ceiling: 12:03 am. That's where I kept my gaze, watching as the seconds ticked away. She hadn't spoken much that night. We had a routine that we stuck to in these sorts of situations and I knew the drill. If she wanted to talk, she would. If she didn't, we'd wake up the next morning and pretend the night prior never happened. My mother even knew the drill. She'd have blueberry pancakes ready for us.

"Have you ever noticed the lights?"

"Huh?"

"The lights, Jane. Have you ever noticed them?"

I genuinely didn't know how to answer the question. I stayed silent as I tried to figure out what she meant.

"The way they look, it's always changing." She sat up. She faced my window, sitting so close to it that her breath began to fog the glass as she spoke in a hushed tone. "Not the stars. The lights. The streetlights, traffic lights, headlights from cars even."

"You're losing me, T. Not that you ever had me in the first place." I laughed.

She didn't. The conversation ended when she said it did and she said it ended right then and there. I didn't prod. The clock struck at 12:10 am before either of us spoke again.

"Goodnight, Jane," Thea said as her head hit the pillow.

"Goodnight T."

I didn't see the light turn green, nor did I put my foot on the gas and turn onto the freeway. At least I don't remember doing any of that. All I remember is that, when the memory ended, I put the car in park. My surroundings had changed but were familiar.

The chain-link fence had been taken down and all that was left was a short concrete block to catch tires. As I turned off my car and stepped out into the just-turned-night air, I stepped over to the edge of the overpass.

The mist clung to the rubber soles of my shoes as I hung my legs over the ledge. At first, my gaze was glued to the sky, looking at the stars. Then Thea's words rang in my head once again. *Not the stars*, she said.

My eyes dropped down to what was below me. The freeway beneath me, the cars whizzing by. People on their way to get somewhere, see someone, do something. Then I caught sight of the lights.

The headlights that shot off in every direction haloed out and burned the night sky out of my eyes. I couldn't see what she saw, at least I don't think I did, but I think I got what she was trying to say in that moment in my bed as she gazed out the window.

There it was. This energy, this something that we couldn't leave alone. We had to harness it, capture it, put it behind glass that distorted it. Then there was the air itself. Flecks of moisture caught it and sent it out in all sorts of directions. Light was something to be claimed, controlled, and yet we never could see it how it wanted to be seen, in its purest form.

I didn't know why she excluded the stars. They suffered the same fate.

Except they weren't put behind glass. They weren't captured to be examined and used. There was something natural, primal about them. Something we couldn't even see in the moment, only long after it had already passed. Perhaps that was the difference between us. Thea was a star; I was a headlight. Perhaps that's why she left and didn't seem to intend on coming back. Perhaps my image was distorted for her too.

Perhaps I was the light among these stars. Distorted by the air, the glass, the eyes of the onlooker. I was something seen on a daily basis but I was something so mundane that I was unrecognizable.

I was far too introspective at this moment and I recognize this now but, at the time, everything had begun to click. The puzzle pieces fell into place and there were a few cutting truths that I could glean.

One: my best friend moved on.

Two: I didn't.

Three: I wasn't the main character of my own life. I was, in fact, the least interesting person in it. I wasn't capable of having these thoughts, only of coming to conclusions I was spoon-fed.

I was a light in a world of stars.

It was at this realization, at this moment of coming to terms with my own mundanity, that I nearly jumped.

Not the happy-go-lucky ending you were looking for, huh?

Well, I will tell you it was only a brief thought. Then it was overpowered by the pondering of what flowers my mother would pick for my funeral, of who would even bother to show up in the first place. But you already know all this if you've taken the time to get this far.

I looked down, saw the ground, and looked right back up. Then down again, this time at my phone, which I hadn't realized was buzzing with an unread notification. The screen, for that moment in time, was a light that my eyes were drawn to. The stars no longer mattered.

"You still coming?" Beckett's message read.

I got up. I brushed myself off. I had my pity party; I was over it. That was the choice I made that day.

"On my way."

The engine started with a roar and my headlights bounced off the misty air. I threw the car into reverse and went back to my mundane little life, the one I almost ended but didn't. No, it didn't end that night.

I like to think it began.

Epilogue

It's not like I've stopped thinking about killing myself. It's that I've realized what everyone will lose if I do. I am the boring one, sure, but I am the observer, the light that illuminates. See what I've managed to do here? I've brought them to life, their stories into the light, just by coming here and seeing you and writing in this stupid little Christmas journal.

What kind of flowers my mom would pick out for the funeral; that's a thought that often pops into my mind, even still. Who would actually bother to show up; that's something I'd really like to know, even now.

She called, can you believe that? Thea wants to grab lunch. I told her I'll let her know when I've got time. We're planning according to *my* schedule.

Oh, the movies I'd miss is another big one still. The movies, the video games, the concerts, the songs, the little things that I take for granted in my life that I would be unable to experience were I no longer living. It's morbid, honestly, thinking about death as a compilation of experiences I'd miss, but it's still how I think about it.

I'm not cured. Don't go patting yourself on the back quite yet. We've still got a long way to go until I get there.

But I'm starting to see that it's inevitable. Things are changing, have been changing for a long time. Right before my eyes, but I guess I wasn't paying close enough attention. I'd spent so much of my teenage life stargazing that I didn't notice that they move, the stars. They drift, they move ever so slightly that it's imperceptible until one night you look up and you're gazing at an entirely new sky.

The constellations you once thought to be a constant fixture having shifted out of sight, ones you'd hardly noticed coming into focus. A lot like people, in a way. At least, some people.

And, who knows, maybe one day you'll glance up and they'll all be back, all the stars you thought you'd lost having returned to just the right spot. Or not. Maybe they'll be a little off, if you're lucky, or they'll be way off to the side or dead center when they'd never been before.

But do these changes make the night sky any less beautiful? Is any one night better than the others? I guess I know the answer.

And yes, I have always despised change. I don't plan on letting myself change completely. I'm still Plain Jane, Jane Doe, Jane Carter. I'm not changing into someone entirely new, just getting a little re-wired is all.

If I'm a light in this world of stars, I better find a power source. Stars are great and all, but if they were enough on their own, we wouldn't have lights. I may not be flashy or exciting, but I'm there. Being extraordinary or interesting has never been my thing, but I think that's okay. I think I'm coming to terms with being mundane but necessary.

It's change, sure, but maybe it's the kind of change that isn't *so* bad.

Cheyenne LaRoque is a University of Southern California alumni and a current MFA candidate at the University of San Francisco. Throughout her academic career, Cheyenne has pushed her own creative boundaries by taking courses in fiction, nonfiction, and poetry. As a student with bills to pay and a second novel in the works, she highly values her downtime. When she isn't busy with school, work, or writing, Cheyenne likes to spend her time playing Dungeons and Dragons or cuddling up with a good book.

Find More of her work here:
CheyenneLaRoque.com